A Calculated Risk

A Deena Powers Mystery

Gloria Getman

Deena Powers Mysteries

by this author

Lottie's Legacy

Birds of a Feather

Published by Squirrel Creek Books
786 Meadow Ave., Exeter, CA 93221

Copyright © 2018 Gloria Getman

This book is a work of fiction. Names, characters, places and incidents are either the product of the author's imagination or are used fictitiously. Any resemblance to actual events, locales, persons, living or dead, is coincidental. The author will assume no responsibility for errors, inaccuracies, omissions, or any inconsistency herein. Any slights related to people, places or organizations are unintentional.

Acknowledgments

A critique group is invaluable to any writer, and so I want to thank my fellow writers the Visalia and Exeter Critique Groups, who have patiently listened during the many sessions and made useful suggestions. Particularly helpful was Roger Boling with his expertise related to police work, guns and ammunition.

Dedication

To Mary Benton

1938 - 2015

RIP

my dear friend

CHAPTER 1

Tony Grimes walked into my office building in Four Creeks on April 14, 2005. I recall the date precisely because I was hunched over my desk working on our income tax return, and it looked like we'd have to file for an extension. I glanced up in time to see him through the front window of the building, and by his purposeful stride across the parking lot, it looked like he was headed in our direction.

So I wasn't surprised when he stepped inside, removed his hat and looked around. I pegged him as a rancher, mid-sixties with long legs and a scowl. He was dressed in a short-sleeved plaid shirt, jeans and dusty boots. He probably had another dozen shirts just like that one, but with different patterns and colors. There was something familiar about his scowl, like maybe I'd seen him before, but I couldn't wrestle up the memory.

He spotted me through the doorway to my office in the back of the room. "Are you Deena Powers?" he asked, then glanced over at Elberta, who was sitting at her desk adjacent to the entrance.

Elberta Simmons is my office assistant, a hefty, big-boned woman whose demeanor might make you wonder if she could be packing a six-gun somewhere on her person. Bert, as she prefers to be called, is invaluable to a short feather-weight like me. I knew she'd seen his approach because she bounced out of her chair the instant Grimes jerked open the outer door. He gave her a shriveling glare.

"It's okay, Bert," I said, still searching my memory banks, knowing I should remember him. I stood and motioned to one of two client chairs positioned in front of my desk. "Yes, I'm Deena Powers. Come in. Have a seat, Mr. . . . . "

"Grimes," he cut in. "Tony Grimes. I've got a problem with a property line, and I want you to prove this well is on my side of it." He stepped forward and laid a snapshot of an irrigation pump on my desk, then dragged a chair over and sat, propping his hat on his knee, the way farmers do when they think the hat is too dirty to put anywhere else, or concerned it might get squashed.

Grimes was not a handsome man. His face looked like a cross between the actor, Lee Marvin, and our neighbor's pit bull. His thin gray hair had a permanent indented line around his head from his wide-brimmed hat. He wasn't wearing glasses, though the indentation on the bridge of his nose indicated he probably needed them for reading.

The instant he'd said his name, it registered, and I recalled what I'd read about a dispute over the well in the local newspaper.

I shuffled my tax papers into a pile and turned my attention to him. "Tell me about your trouble, Mr. Grimes."

He proceeded to explain that a woman by the name of Casitas Brown had recently purchased a swath of land next to his in the south end of the county and was claiming his well was actually on her side of the property line.

There's nothing more precious in the Central Valley of California than water and water rights, and over the years an enormous amount of money has been spent in court battles to protect it.

Casitas Brown, I later learned, had been born in a isolated desert town with a questionable reputation. She'd grown up rough and rich due to her mother's choice of profession.

"I don't know where she got that idea," he continued, "but now she's set her sights on my well. She's saying the line was fudged when my great-grandpa, Fillmore Winton Grimes, filed his homestead back in the early days of this county. I want you to prove her wrong. I've got an expensive lawyer and we'll be going to court over this. I've waited years to develop that acreage because of the lack of water. My granddad, Willard Grimes, dry-farmed winter wheat on it, but that's not possible anymore. Not enough rainfall. It cost me near five-hundred-thousand to get at water that deep. It's my land and my water, and I don't aim to have it stolen from me." His face had gone from a ruddy tan to a blotchy red while he talked.

"The deed must have been recorded," I said. "It can't be too hard to find."

Grimes shifted his weight. "That's the rub. Back in the early days, this area was part of Mariposa County. It was broken up into various counties, Delta being one of them. Some land records didn't get transferred like they should have. No telling where they ended up. I want you to find the one that was my great-grandfather's."

He reached into his shirt pocket and pulled out a piece of paper. "I've got some business to attend to in Arizona. I'll be away at least a week. I brought a check. This ought to cover your time and expenses while I'm gone. I'll expect an accounting, of course. You can contact my daughter if you need help with family background, names and such."

He laid a check and a business card on my desk. I picked up the card. It had a single name on it, Claudine, as if the world ought to know who she was. I did.

Claudine Morales was a well-known artist whose work had been featured, not only in her local gallery in the city of Delta, but in upscale galleries all over Southern California. I'd purchased one of her paintings myself. She was married to Rick Morales, a real estate broker, who'd made a ton of money during the housing boom.

I remembered hearing that Claudine's father was reputed to own farms in several states, but until that

4

minute hadn't made the connection. He was a hands-on guy who flew his own plane to save time traveling to manage his vast ag business.

Mr. Grimes glanced at his watch. I noted that it wasn't a Rolex, though he certainly could have afforded one. More likely he simply wasn't one to spend money on glitzy nonessentials.

"I've got to get going," he said. "I have an appointment in Phoenix this afternoon. I'll contact you when I return."

"May I ask why you picked me out of all the investigators in this county?" Since I'd spent both time and money attracting attention to my recently opened agency, I wanted to know what had been most effective.

He rose from the chair and banged his hat against his knee. "I've met your husband."

I would have preferred his reason had been because of some glowing referral, but due to the size of the retainer and the tax bill I had on my mind, I didn't complain. I stood. "We need a contract if I'm to work for you."

"Right now, a handshake is good enough for me." He stretched across the desk to offer his hand. "I've arranged for my office girl to bring you a file later this afternoon," he said as I took his hand. "Give her the papers, and I'll sign them when I return." With a half-hearted wave, he moved to leave.

After the outer door closed, Bert appeared, leaned against the door frame and raised a sculpted eyebrow. "So that's Tony Grimes," she said. "A rare sighting. Who knew?"

I waved the check. "Well, this ought to keep us in jelly doughnuts for a while."

She laughed. "I have a hunch you're going to earn every one of those gooey treats. I've heard he's not a patient man."

I slipped the check into my desk drawer and turned my attention to the urgent task before me—sorting through a pile of receipts to locate a few more deductions. Bert went back to transcribing hand-written notes I'd made about a crack in the sidewalk outside city hall. I'd been contacted by the city attorney the week before and asked to look into a complaint from a local woman. She had stated she tripped on the crack and injured her knee. The notes described what I'd found when I went to the site, taken photos and made measurements.

At noon, I piled all the papers into a folder and put them in my desk drawer. We hung a sign on the door and went around the corner to our favorite lunch spot, Paco's Grill. Paco makes a mean enchilada I enjoy, spiced right for an American palate.

We were seated in a booth, and I'd nearly finished my lunch when the TV that hung from the ceiling in the corner flashed breaking news on the screen. A single engine Piper Cherokee PA-28 owned by the Grimes Corporation had crashed after taking off from the ag airfield near Grimes' south county headquarters. Anthony Winton Grimes was dead. I stared at the screen in disbelief, my mouth hanging open. Tony Grimes didn't get rich by being careless. What could possibly have gone wrong?!

CHAPTER 2

I paid the tab and we headed back to the office. My lunch wasn't settling well. It's jarring when someone you know dies suddenly, even if it's someone you just met. It leaves one feeling unsettled, vulnerable, and cognizant that life is uncertain. In this case, my natural sympathy for the Grimes family was tempered by my disappointment at having lost the opportunity to work for Tony Grimes. A satisfactory outcome could have led to referrals, something I needed if my agency was going to thrive.

"I guess you can kiss that check goodbye," Bert said as I unlocked and opened the door. "I bet the CFO at the Grimes Corporation will call, telling you they'll send someone to pick it up."

"You're probably right." I heaved a sigh and reached to disable the security alarm. In the few months since I'd set up my business, Grimes had been my most promising client. Background checks, process serving and witness location would barely pay the rent.

I returned to my desk to continue sorting receipts. Besides procrastination, my tax issue was related to the sale the previous year of the office building I'd owned in southern California. The profit might have been offset by the cost of opening my new office, except that the expense had actually occurred in the current year. I'd taken my problem to an accountant I knew the week before. He said he wasn't a magician and chided me for waiting so long.

A half-hour later, I'd reached the bottom of the shoebox and grumbled under my breath, vowing to be better organized before the next tax season.

Truth is, I'd never quite achieved my former sense of order since getting married to Buzz Walker and having a baby. I confess I never imagined I would become a mother at my age. Statistics were against it. But life can be full of surprises.

Moving to Four Creeks was something else I never imagined either. For the record, Four Creeks is situated in the southern part of the San Joaquin Valley not far from a popular national park. At last count it had a population of around eight thousand. It's known as the orange belt because, due to the mild winters and hot summers, the area produces an immense amount of oranges. It's the blistering hot summers that test my mettle, but as the old adage goes, bloom where you are planted, and that's what I planned to do.

Before our daughter, Peggy Lou, was born, Buzz and I decided I would set aside my career to be a full-time mother—at least for her first three years. I reveled in watching her growth and development, but by the time her second birthday rolled around, I concluded that after decades of city living, I wasn't cut out for the solitary life of a good ranch-wife. Even though the countryside where our ranch is located is beautiful in the spring, I'd have to admit there were days when I felt like singing the theme song from the old TV show Green Acres.

Interacting with a couple of horses, my Doberman, Jeff, and my beloved two-year-old didn't measure up to a complex conversation with other adults. In spite of what I'd heard from friends about how hard it was to manage a career and motherhood, I was full of confidence. So as soon as Peggy Lou turned three, I set out to find a good nursery school and leased a board-and-batten building on the east end of Main Street in Four Creeks.

I'm not sure Buzz ever understood my state-of-mind, but he did acknowledge that our daughter needed to learn how to get along with other children before she started school.

The thing I hadn't considered was Aunt Madge's point of view. Madge, my dad's sister, has been the closest thing I've had to family in recent years. From the time my mom died when I was seven, she did her best to fill the void. Even though we aren't related by blood—I was adopted—it didn't matter to her. The summers I spent with her and Uncle Henry were the best a kid could ask for. And since then, she's seen me through several rough spots: divorce, a jarring job loss, and more recently, the death of my dad.

The instant Madge learned we'd decided to honor her by naming our daughter Margaret Louise, she took on an attitude of ownership. I won't say she interferes, but she never hesitates to offer her advice. She said it seemed a big name for such a little girl. Hence, the nickname—Peggy Lou.

Still, her reaction to my plan was a bit of a surprise when I went to visit the week after Peggy Lou's birthday. She pulled out a chair at the dining room table and sat to listen while I described the attributes of Happy Trails Nursery School. As I expanded on what I had in mind, she got that look she gets when she's about to launch an argument, a slight scowl and pinched lips.

Half way through my explanation, she said, "Nursery school and then a babysitter in the afternoon?" Her brow furrowed. "I agree she needs to learn to interact with other children, but the very idea of some stranger caring for my namesake will never do. I'll pick her up and take care of her after school," she said in a no nonsense tone. "Except for the days Wilbur and I go to Golden Hills Care Home to visit, she can have lunch with me and take her nap here."

What she had proposed was very generous. It meant she'd be giving up some of her usual social activities. It also meant that when Wilbur, Madge's long-haired Chihuahua, fulfilled his comfort dog role, I'd either have to take the afternoon off, or take Peggy Lou to the office with me. I was mulling over how I'd work it out when Madge's voice penetrated my mental hopscotch.

"But I still don't agree with the notion that you have to work," she said.

"A year in a good college rivals the cost of a Mazerati these days. Whatever profit I make will go into Peggy's college fund."

She drew in a deep breath. "I see your point." She looked at me over her glasses. "But you won't be doing anything dangerous will you?"

CHAPTER 3

"I'm going to walk over to the post office to get the mail." Bert plucked the P.O. box key from the fancy covered candy dish where we kept it.

"Okay. I guess I've done all I can with this." I heaved a sigh and gathered the clutter of tax information into a folder ready to take it across town to my accountant. As I pulled my handbag out of the desk drawer, my cell phone jingled. It was Aunt Madge.

"Peggy Lou just woke up from her nap," she said. "I think she has a fever. Her cheeks are flushed, and her forehead seems overly warm."

"It's probably another ear infection." I glanced at the time—three o'clock. "Drat it. It's been one thing after another ever since she started nursery school—colds, pin worms, ear infections...."

"It's not unusual when children start school," Madge said. "I'll give her a tepid bath. That should reduce her fever."

"Okay. I'll be there in half an hour." I disconnected, stood and muttered an expletive. "I'm going to drop this stuff off at the accountant's, then pick up Peggy Lou from Madge's. She's sick again."

Gloria Getman

"Oh, golly. I'm sorry," Bert said with a look of concern.

I looped my purse strap over my shoulder. "If she's not better in the morning, I may have to take her to the pediatrician. I'll text you if that happens."

Later that evening, I sat by her bed with a cool washcloth in my hand and stared at my daughter. Her fever had finally broken and she was asleep. Buzz stood behind me.

"Maybe I should take her out of nursery school," I said.

"You can't keep her in a bubble."

"Why not?"

Peggy Lou wasn't his first child. He had a grown daughter from his previous marriage, so he'd been through childhood illnesses before. I'd read a dozen books on child care, but found all the advice rang hollow when it came to real life.

I pushed out of the chair and hunched my shoulders in an attempt to stretch out the kinks of tension. Buzz ran his hand up and down my neck, then massaged my shoulder muscles.

"Mmmm. Keep that up and I'll follow you anywhere."

He chuckled. "Come on. Let's go to bed." He took my hand and pulled me toward the door. "I've got something in mind."

As soon as we were settled in bed, Buzz leaned over, nuzzled my hair, and gently nibbled my earlobe.

"How'd you meet Tony Grimes?" I asked, pretending to ignore him.

He propped on one elbow and looked at me. "Yeah. I heard about the crash. Terrible. I met Grimes years ago when his son was having some difficulty. I talked him out of making a bad decision."

"Which was?"

Buzz lay back on his pillow. "It's a long story."

I rolled over on my side. "I'm listening."

"The boy and a couple of his buds were whooping it up in the park in town. One of the neighbors called the station, complaining. I was on patrol that night, my first week with the Four Creeks PD, and went to check it out. They had a boom-box blaring, beer cans scattered around on the grass, and they were loaded. They were celebrating the Grimes kid's eighteenth birthday, they said. He was due to leave for college the next week.

"I made them clean up the park, and while they were doing that, I checked for wants and warrants. The boys had clean records, so I hauled them in and had them call their parents. In those days cops had a lot more leeway than they do now.

"The parents of the two local kids came to get them. But Mr. Grimes was so infuriated, he wanted his son to stay in jail overnight. The county jail was no place for that boy, not with some of the rough characters we'd put there that week. I talked him into picking up his kid, and knowing he owned a ranch, suggested he make him work off his hangover. He did, and later called to thank me."

I leaned over and kissed him on the cheek. "You're a good cop."

"Yeah, yeah. I'll bet you say that to all the guys with a badge." He scowled. "How'd you find out I knew Tony Grimes?"

"He came to my office today. He wanted me to search for his great-grandfather's earliest land claim. A woman bought the land next to his and is now claiming the well he recently put in is on her side of the line."

Buzz gave a low whistle. "I'll bet that went over big. Wells south of here cost a fortune to sink." He scratched the side of his neck. "I have no personal experience to draw on, but I've heard that Grimes is, or was, like a raging bull when crossed.

"I wonder what will happen now that he's dead."

"A lot of lawyers and a lot of haggling, I imagine." Buzz reached over and turned out the light, then moved close and slid his hand along my hip.

The first voice I heard in the morning was that of my daughter. "Mommy. Bekfust. Peggy hungee."

I pried open one eye. The room was bathed in dim light. Standing on my side of the bed was the kid who'd

16

seemed so ill the night before, now clear-eyed and hugging her favorite stuffed toy kitten. The kitten had led a rough life. It's fur was no longer white and was missing in some spots. One day after she dropped it in the toilet, I'd had to give it a bath. But it's condition didn't matter to her. She carried the wretched thing everywhere, with the exception of nursery school. Her teacher took one look at it and wouldn't allow it in the building.

I glanced over my shoulder and saw the other half of the bed was empty. Buzz had no doubt fed his horses and left for his shift. In the last year, he had gone to work for the Sheriff's Department in hopes of better pay and benefits, and now was in a position that often required overtime.

Reluctant to get up, I lifted the blanket, an invitation for Peggy Lou to climb in next to me. "Let's snuggle for a little bit."

She didn't need coaxing. She liked snuggling. We lay spoon-fashion while I enjoyed the warmth of her little body next to me.

Three minutes passed.

"Peggy hungee," she repeated.

I pulled back the covers and twenty minutes later, we were washed, brushed, combed, and dressed. Sitting in her highchair, Peggy Lou was spooning some unhealthy puffed cereal into her mouth, and I was sipping a hot cup of coffee from the pot Buzz had prepared and left for me. Love that guy.

CHAPTER 4

The next week went by in a blur. Besides the usual duties of a working mother, I had been contacted by a couple of local businessmen to do background checks on prospective employees. In addition, the city's problem with the sidewalk crack wasn't resolved. The attorney wanted me to interview two witnesses the woman claimed saw her fall.

Then on the Monday after Tony Grimes' funeral, I got a phone call from a woman who said she was calling me on behalf of Claudine Morales. She said that Claudine wanted to meet with me in Delta at the office of Clifford Jessup, the attorney for the Grimes Corporation. I figured she wanted me to return the check Tony Grimes had left with me, so I agreed. I scribbled the address on a message pad and we settled on a 1 o'clock appointment.

During the fifteen mile drive that afternoon, I thought over the last time I'd seen Claudine. I'd been walking past her gallery on my way to a grocery store nearby, when I saw a six-by-eight inch painting of a little girl and her puppy through the gallery window. Struck by the resemblance to Peggy Lou, I couldn't pass by without a closer look. I walked in, and as I stood studying it, the breathy voice of a woman asked, "You like it?"

"I do," I said, not turning around. "She looks so much like my two-year-old. How much is it?"

When she stated the price, I couldn't suppress a slight gasp, stepped back, and started to mumble my way out of the purchase. I turned, thinking I'd make a quick departure, and recognized Claudine from newspaper photos. Taller than me by several inches, her honey-colored hair hung almost to her waist. She was wearing a loose white blouse, a colorful ankle-length skirt and matching sandals.

She smiled a knowing smile. "What's your little girl's name?"

I told her, my eyes likely still registering sticker shock.

She swept her hair back over her shoulders. "You know, I've had that piece hanging there for six months, and you're the only person who has seemed interested in it." She took the painting off the hook. "I think it's time I discounted it." She named a price, much lower than the original.

I'd been ready to run out the door. I swallowed. "I'll take it," I said, knowing I'd have to explain the bulge on our credit card statement to Buzz.

All the way home that day, I pondered the transaction. I doubted the painting had been on display very long. Her work was too popular for that to happen. I'd never know why she'd discounted it for me, except perhaps, just a simple kindness.

I pulled into a three-story parking tower not far from the Front Street address and hoofed it the short distance. The building was a utilitarian type built in the early '80s, a square box, sheathed in pebblestone, with a wrought iron railing on the stairs to the second floor, my destination. My footsteps echoed along the vinyl tile in the vacant hall.

I spotted Clifford Jessup's name in gold lettering on a door and opened it, surprised to see the interior was vastly different compared to the outer spaces. Textured, peppermint-green wall covering and embossed draperies gave the room an upscale tone. Padded chairs were positioned around a low table that held several artsy magazines, and soft music played in the background. A dark-haired receptionist, perhaps thirty-five, sat behind a handsome oak desk, a computer in front of her. The green blouse, underneath her dark blue suit jacket, was the same shade as the wall covering. I couldn't help but wonder how long she'd searched to find a shirt to match the décor.

She smiled and rose from her chair. "Ms. Powers?"

I returned her smile. "That's me," I said and stepped forward.

"You're expected. This way." She motioned to a door to the right of her desk and moved to open it.

As I approached the open doorway, I could see Clifford Jessup, a bushy-haired man with eyebrows to match, seated behind a dark mahogany desk only slightly smaller than Aunt Madge's dining room table. It held a telephone and a folder, but was otherwise bare, the sunlight from a large window on his left reflecting off the polished surface. Maybe the expanse of the desk represented his importance or the fees he charged.

I stepped into the room. Claudine Morales was sitting in a leather client chair, positioned adjacent to the big desk, her right arm resting on it. She was dressed in the same skirt and blouse she'd been wearing that day in her gallery. A small handbag lay in her lap.

The stress of her father's death was evident in her sallow complexion and the dark circles around her eyes. In addition, her honey-colored hair appeared to have lost its sheen. Her body language, sagging shoulders and drooping mouth, said her energy level was waning.

Jessup rose as I approached them. I pegged him at mid-forties, five ten, maybe 180 pounds. He was dressed in a suit I guessed might be an Armani, something not seen much in this area. The quality of his shirt and tie, likewise.

We shook hands all around and he indicated the other client chair, then resumed his position behind the desk.

I sat and offered condolence, directing my attention to Claudine. "I was stunned by what happened," I said, "especially since your father had left my office only a few hours earlier."

Claudine nodded and thanked me, tears glistening in her eyes. She took a deep breath as if to gather enough energy to continue. "I asked you to come because I want to talk to you about his reason for contacting you."

I opened my handbag. "I brought the check. I expected that you'd want it returned, under the circumstances."

She held up her hand as if warding off something unpleasant. A tear escaped her right eye and trickled down her cheek. "I'm sorry," she said. She reached in her purse and pulled out a tissue.

Jessup cleared his throat. "What Claudine is trying to convey is that the family doesn't want to terminate the investigation Mr. Grimes proposed. The problem of the unfounded allegation of property line falsification has not gone away. Consequently, we—I mean, the family wishes you to proceed."

Claudine wiped her eyes, sniffled into the tissue and nodded. "Daddy was so upset over that awful woman's claim that he hired a detective in Bakersfield to investigate her. He learned she has a very seedy background." She went on to relate the degree of seediness. "We just can't let her get away with it. That land is part of our family heritage."

Jessup broke in. "I've prepared a contract." He opened the folder, pulled out a sheaf of papers and separated it into two parts. "We simply need to fill in a few blanks."

I smiled. Employment is good, especially when it involves a law firm well known in the community. I told him my hourly rate and he filled in a space.

"May I see the check, so I can record the amount of the retainer?" He held out his hand, expectantly.

I passed it to him.

When he saw what it said, an "Ummm," came from his lips as if he was about to protest the generous sum.

Claudine stretched her arm across the desk and touched the side of his hand with her index finger, a gesture that smacked of intimacy.

The faintest nod of assent followed and he recorded the amount, then turned both copies around in my direction. He held out the pen, which I took, and scanned the document to be sure it covered my expenses before signing and dating it in the appropriate places. He then folded one copy, placed it in an envelope and passed it to me. "Any other expenses related to the investigation and the final accounting will be handled by this office."

Claudine straightened in her chair. "My brother, Fillmore, has information about the property and the well. He's been handling much of the California operation for some time." She pulled a business card out of her purse and leaned forward to hand it to me.

I nodded. "Thanks. I may want to see the location of the well in question." I rose from the chair. I wanted to ask if the authorities had conveyed the result of the investigation of the crash, but held back.

As if reading my thoughts, she said, "The day after the accident, Fillie called me and said that a man from the NTSB office in Gateway came right out and took a couple dozen pictures of my father's plane, poked around some, and then told him he could move the wreckage to the hanger at the ranch. We haven't heard anything since then. It's tearing me up."

Cliff Jessup got out of his chair, walked around and stood behind Claudine. He put one hand on her shoulder. "This has been very hard on the family, not knowing what happened. I'm a licensed pilot, and I don't know why it's taking so long to get a conclusion from the investigator. I could understand it if it were a huge airliner, but this was just a small aircraft."

Claudine dabbed her nose again. "I can't stop thinking about it. Daddy was such a careful pilot, it seems inconceivable he would make some clumsy mistake. And weather wasn't an issue. The only other thing would be something wrong with the plane, but he'd never tolerate any maintenance left neglected." She chewed on one of her nails, her sculpted brows drawn together.

I wasn't sure how to respond. When my friend, Boots, had had a bad landing at the airfield in Santa Barbara, I learned that the NTSB doesn't spend a lot of money on small plane crash investigations. They tend to assume that the cause is either weather or pilot error—something the pilot failed to check. They rarely consider a mechanical malfunction unless it's obvious.

As I picked up my bag, I paused. "If you don't get a definitive answer, you could hire a private investigator who specializes in accidents of that nature. I could give you the names of a couple I know. "

Claudine looked up at me, eyes widened. "Yes," she said. "I suppose we could. Thank you for mentioning it." For the first time that day, I saw a weak smile.

I offered my hand to each of them. "I'll be in touch as soon as I have something to report." As I left the room, I glanced back. Jessup was still standing with his hand on her shoulder.

CHAPTER 5

On the walk back to my car, I considered the scene I'd left behind. I normally try not to draw conclusions without ample evidence, but in this case, it was hard to miss the touching attorney-client relationship. I decided not to give it much thought, since it wouldn't affect my assignment.

I got into the Explorer, exited the parking facility, then circled the block in order to make an easy entrance onto the freeway and headed east.

The drive from Delta to Four Creeks in April makes possible a view of the snow-crested Sierras that may be the best in the state. The previous day a weak weather front had moved through, leaving a few sprinkles and the sky crystal-clear. Spring in this part of the valley only lasts about six weeks. The fact that before long high pressure would take over and valley haze would prevail made me savor the view even more than usual.

It was almost three o'clock when I turned off the highway onto the two-lane road leading into Four Creeks. Traffic in town is generally heavier at that time of day, but finding a parking spot is a snap compared to

Ortega Bay where I had my business before moving to the ranch.

I stopped at the bank to deposit the retainer check I could legitimately claim now that I had a contract. Since the post office was right next door, I walked over to pick up the mail, something Bert would normally do. But she had called that morning to say she needed the day off. She'd joined a hiking group, and after a weekend outing her muscles were calling for more time to recover.

I hadn't been thinking about hiring an office assistant until the day Bert walked in that first week. She introduced herself and said Sam Strickland, the owner of a large detective agency in Delta encouraged her to talk to me. She'd worked for him for ten years, she said, but recently decided she wanted more free time for her hobbies. That suited me just fine. I told her I wasn't sure how much work I'd have for her.

After the usual background check, I contacted her the next day, and we agreed on a flexible schedule. Boxes of supplies from the storage unit where I'd kept the furnishings from my old office were still unpacked, so she'd been a big help getting organized.

From the bank to my office building was a two-minute drive. Once inside, I stood over the wastebasket and dropped in the junk-mail: a pizza ad, an invitation to have my hearing checked, and an urgent plea to upgrade my cable TV service. That left the Edison bill, which I tossed on my desk, and then turned on the computer.

When the hard drive booted up, I opened one of the forms I'd created and logged the basic information about the new assignment, then made a list of sources I planned to use. I was thinking it ought to be a slam-dunk, but something told me it wasn't going to be that easy. If it were, Tony Grimes wouldn't have shown up at my door; his secretary could have located the information for him.

Curious about the organization, I typed the Grimes name into my favorite search engine. A lengthy article about the Grimes Corporation made interesting reading. Their vast holdings were divided between Arizona and California with the headquarters maintained locally. The corporate board was made up of Tony Grimes, both his children, Fillmore and Claudine, plus two others, Willard Grimes and Vivian Rudd, Tony's siblings. The spouses were also included.

The piece continued and listed the various crops grown by the corporation: alfalfa, citrus, wine grapes, kiwis, and walnuts. It mentioned a few of the labor troubles they'd had over the years, and concluded with the many organizations in which the family patriarch, Tony, was involved: the Farm Bureau, Wine Growers Association, Citrus Mutual and a couple others. It concluded by elaborating about how the Grimes family had been pioneers in this part of the valley and had passed their holdings down to the next generation, finally incorporating in the late 1940s.

There was also a link to an old newspaper article about Willard Grimes, referred to as Will by most people, and how he'd become involved in an altercation at a Farm Bureau meeting two years previous. The two men had gotten into a shouting match during the meeting. Will had waited for the other man outside, punched him in the face and threatened him with a tire iron. A witness called the cops. The article didn't report the cause of the argument or if any charges were filed.

Another article related the corporation's generous support of the local 4H Club. There were a few others, but when I looked up, it was past four. My search had taken up more time than a Parisian lunch. I needed to pick up Peggy Lou at Madge's house. I created a folder in the computer, saved a copy of the first document, plus a few pages from another, logged off and locked up.

Peggy Lou was perched on her knees at the dining room table with a coloring book in front of her when I walked in. Wilbur greeted me with rousing barks and scampered around my feet, stopping long enough to bounce in the air a couple of times. I leaned over and ruffled his fur.

"Mommy!" Peggy Lou slid off the chair and ran to wrap her arms around my legs. "Did you bring me a new book?"

"Not this time, honey."

Madge was in the kitchen, stirring something on the stove that smelled like spaghetti sauce. I sat on the chair with Peggy on my lap. She'd been decorating a dinosaur with her crayons. She hadn't mastered the skill of staying within the lines yet, so the smiling creature looked like he was leaking purple skin. Since she'd never seen a real dinosaur, how would she know what color it should be? Come to think of it, I'd never seen a real one either. I had to take someone else's word for it. I picked up a green crayon and filled in a couple of the leaves on a tree.

"I've been hired to do a property search for the Grimes Corporation," I said over my shoulder to Madge.

"Isn't that the purpose of a title insurance company?"

I rose from the chair, put Peggy Lou down to continue her artistry, and went to sit on one of the stools at the counter that separates the dining room from Madge's kitchen.

"In this case, the property was acquired in the early days of the county by an ancestor. From what I hear, records from those times might take some time to locate."

"The county records office ought to be a help."

"I hope so."

I noticed Madge looked a little pale. She was normally a bundle of energy. Besides getting up early and doing all her housework before noon, she was active in several organizations like the Garden Club, Women of Colonial Heritage, and Comfort Dog Owners. I wondered if babysitting every afternoon might be getting to be too much for her, but I didn't want to ask her about it in front of Peggy Lou.

I returned to stand behind my daughter. "Let's put the crayons away now. We need to get home and get dinner started."

A whimper came from the recipient of my directive. Not wanting to risk a battle of wills, I opted for bribery. "We can stop at the bookstore on the way home. I think I saw a book about a dinosaur in the window." I stole a glance at my aunt. She was scowling. Madge doesn't believe in bribery. It worked, though. Peggy cheerfully gathered the crayons and coloring book and hurried to place them on the shelf in Madge's bookcase.

The bookstore was situated in the center of town. My normal route home from Madge's was to turn right at the bottom of Indian Hill and head straight north to the highway. Though the bookstore was out of my way, I figured I'd better keep my part of the bargain with my daughter. I parked the SUV in front and helped Peggy out of her car seat.

Inside, I led her to the children's section. She pulled two books from the shelf, awkwardly turning them over and around to view the front and back. "This one?" she asked, looking up at me.

"Not for your grade level," I responded. I returned them to the shelf and showed her the book I had in mind, *The Happy Dinosaur*. The store provided a short-legged table, painted orange, and a couple of matching chairs for children. Peggy Lou settled on one of the chairs and began turning pages.

"Stay here," I told her. "Mommy's going to look at books too." I walked to the non-fiction section with county history in mind. The shelf held a half-dozen volumes related to farming in California, and just as many about local water problems.

"Well, if it isn't Deena Powers," a voice behind me said. "I haven't seen much of you since you married Lieutenant Walker. Noticed you opened an office over by the doughnut shop. How's business?"

I don't know what it is about Sheila Deiter, but she always makes me grit my teeth. Maybe it's her eager-beaver attitude, or maybe something I hadn't defined yet. I pasted on a smile and turned to face her. She was wearing jeans and an aqua-blue cotton blouse that suited her coloring. Her hair was the same shade of blonde with highlights. She'd put on a little weight, but not enough to do her any harm. "Hi. Still working for the newspaper?"

"Of course," she said with a lift of her chin like I ought to have known it. "I covered a very important story, the plane crash that killed that big-wig farmer."

"Sorry, I didn't see the article." It was a lie. I had seen it and the pictures. She'd done a superb job on the report.

"Too bad. My feature was first rate, even if I do say so myself. By the time I arrived, they'd already removed the body from the wreckage and were leaving with it. I wasn't allowed to get close to the plane, but I hung around to watch the guy from the NTSB take pictures. Got a few good ones myself. He had a lot of questions for the old guy's son. Even at a distance, I got the sense his questions made him uncomfortable. From what I overheard, the son sure was in a hurry to get the plane carted back to the hanger at their airfield. I kept thinking, what's with him? I'd sure like to find out what caused that crash."

"I imagine the family'd like to have the same information. " I glanced around to see what Peggy Lou was doing.

"I wonder who's going to inherit the farm, so to speak," she said.

"It's a corporation and will likely continue to operate as always."

"But I'll bet there's going to be a power struggle."

"It's possible, I guess." She was beginning to get on my nerves, always trying to find a story in other people's tragedies.

Peggy Lou picked a second book off the shelf and brought it to me. "I want this one too."

I shook my head. "Only one book."

Peggy's mouth turned down in the beginnings of a pout.

"Is this your little girl?" Sheila asked. "She's a doll." She knelt down to be at eye level with her. "Whatcha got there? Oooh. Pretty books. Let me see." She took both of the books from Peggy's hands and held them up to view the covers. "A dinosaur or a pony. Which is your favorite?"

Peggy pointed to the pony.

"Good choice. That's the one you should have." Sheila handed the books back to her and stood.

Peggy held up her choice. "This one, Mommy."

Sheila grinned. "Problem solved," she said with an air of superiority.

Leave it to a stranger to charm my child and keep her from making a scene. I took my daughter by the hand and led her to the checkout, where I pulled out my credit card.

A couple of minutes later, Peggy Lou was carrying her book in a bag and we were headed for the exit. As we passed by Sheila, who held the latest political best-seller in her hand, Peggy Lou gave her a big smile and a goodbye wave. Sheila returned the gesture.

"I like that lady," my daughter said with enthusiasm as we went out the door.

CHAPTER 6

I was late getting to the office the next morning because my daughter had decided to display her growing independence by arguing about which shirt to wear. With a stomp of her foot, she insisted on a sleeveless blue shirt that was too thin for the overcast morning. After a demonstration of mommy-power, a compromise was struck. She wore a cotton sweater over it. Our little disagreement was soon forgotten on the way to town, and by the time I parked in front of her pre-school she was wiggling, eager to get out and see her friends.

During the four-block drive to the office, I shifted my focus to the work I hoped to accomplish that day. As I unlocked the door, I heard the phone ringing, rushed to disable the alarm and grab the receiver. A gravelly female voice at the other end of the line identified herself and asked if I was available to search for her dog, a Pekinese that had escaped from her yard during the night. In the nicest way I could, I explained that I sometimes searched for people, but not dogs. I sympathized with her, recalling how when my Dobe, Jeff, first moved to Buzz's ranch, he would wander off into the surrounding fields, leaving me worried he might meet up with a rattlesnake and not recognize the danger. Up until then, he had been a city dog. It took weeks for him to adjust to his new boundaries.

I'd barely finished the conversation, when Bert limped in. I was at the mini-kitchenette in the corner, one I'd had built to serve as a place to make coffee and store snacks in an under-counter fridge. I glanced in her direction. By the way she moved, it was obvious her muscles hadn't fully recovered from her strenuous weekend. Having felt similar strains after my first Pilates class a few years back, I could identify with her discomfort.

"Did you try hot and cold compresses on those complaining muscles?" I asked over my shoulder as I finished filling the coffee pot and started it gurgling.

She lowered herself onto her desk chair. "Yes. I used hot and cold, plus Emu cream and even resorted to some horse liniment my neighbor had. It's going to take a lot more conditioning before I sign up for another hike like that one. Did you know that coming down a mountain trail is just as hard as going up?"

"I've heard that. I suppose you have blisters too."

"Oh, yes, but my calves aren't quite as sore this morning. I figured lying around the house thinking about my decrepit state wasn't going to help. Coming to work would, at the least, be distracting."

The phone rang and Bert reached for the receiver. After a greeting, she swiveled her chair in my direction.

"Hold on." She put her thumb over the little speaker port. "This is Judy Amrine. She says she needs to speak to you about something important."

Judy had been my assistant when I had my business in Ortega Bay. After years of working together, we'd become good friends, but there were miles between us now. She'd retired to be near family in San Diego, and I hadn't heard from her since the holidays.

Leaving the door to my office open, I hurried to slide into my desk chair to take the call. "Hi. How are you?"

"Loving life. Hey, I hate to be the bearer of bad tidings, but I just heard on the TV news that Buck Harper escaped from prison last night. I could hardly believe my ears. I had no idea he was down here at Centinela. They'll probably pick him up before nightfall, but I thought you ought to know. Does his sister still live in Four Creeks?"

It was just like Judy not to beat around the bush when she had something to say. It was one of the things I liked about her.

"She's only his half-sister," I replied, "but as far as I know, she still lives here, though I haven't seen her lately. I doubt he'd come up this way. He'd be a fool. He's more likely to head down into Mexico, if he gets a chance."

"You're probably right, but watch your back anyway. How's the little one?"

We chatted a couple of minutes about family matters before disconnecting with promises to stay in touch.

Bert came to the doorway of my office with a mug of coffee in each hand. She set one of the mugs on my desk. "It's none of my business, but who's heading to Mexico? Are you in some danger?"

I shook my head. "Unlikely." I launched into a description of how, seven years earlier, Buck Harper had caused the death of my dad by running my car off the road, and later, at the behest of another scum-bag, had tried to kill me by dumping me in an icy river out in Sandy Cove. "He didn't stop there either. He smashed through Madge's front door intent on bashing in my head with the tire iron he carried. He's a vicious creature, a career criminal whose been incarcerated ever since."

I picked up the cup, took a sip and reached to turn on my computer. In the last few years, I'd finally gotten past the nightmares about the incident, so to have that name intrude did jangle a nerve. I tried not to let on. "He won't get far. Judy's right. He'll be back in custody before midnight."

I took a second swallow of coffee. "I have some good news." To change the subject, I told her about my appointment with Claudine Morales and the contract I'd received.

"That's terrific," Bert said, likely envisioning regular work for herself as a result.

I fished the Grimes Corporation business card out of my desk drawer and laid it on the surface. "I'm going to see if I can connect with Fillmore Grimes. I expect he has the property records I'll need. And if he knows about when his ancestor acquired the land, that would help too." I reached for the desk phone and peered at the tiny print on the card. Reading glasses were probably in my near future.

A soft-sounding female voice answered. I told her my name and stated the reason for my call. She put me on hold and after a brief period, Fillmore Grimes came on the line.

"My sister told me you'd be getting in touch," he said. "I have some things I need to attend to this afternoon. If you want to drive out here to the headquarters this morning, I have time."

We agreed on ten o'clock and he gave me directions.

The county courthouse was next on my list of contacts. If Tony Grimes was right about some early records being mislaid, I needed to know. The internet gave me the phone number, and when my call was answered by a cheerful voice, I explained I wanted to find out the year of earliest land records recorded in the county.

"You need the Recorder's office," she said. "I'll transfer your call." A moment later, I explained my mission to another woman.

"You mean you want to know the date of the earliest deeds," she said with a tinge of annoyance in her voice.

"Yes."

"I can't tell you that. You'll have to come in and look for yourself."

Her response puzzled me. Thinking I hadn't explained well enough, I said, "I don't need the exact date at this point. If you could give me a ballpark estimate of the year, that would do."

"I'm sorry. I can't tell you. You'll have to come in."

Irritation crawled up the back of my neck. I said thank you, though I didn't mean it, and disconnected. She must have known. How could she work there and not know? Sheesh!

I returned to the internet for a search of county history. Several sites were informative though none of them gave the precise information I wanted, dates of the earliest land ownership. One listed several names of pioneer settlers and their locations, even the year of their arrival. Reading about them was interesting, but no real help.

The sky was still overcast when I turned right off the highway southwest of town. I glanced at the odometer, noting the mileage, and wished I had a GPS. At the time my dad purchased the Explorer I still drove, he didn't think the device was worth the expense. He knew Ortega county like the back of his hand. My situation was different. I was unfamiliar with many of the roads in the area, so a GPS was something I'd be shopping for very soon.

Fillmore had said to turn south in another four miles. After making the turn, the landscape changed from open fields to walnut groves on either side. After a couple of minutes I came to a place where the road split, a branch going off through the orchard. He hadn't mentioned anything about another turn, so I continued on, avoiding ruts in the road, and a minute or two later came to a dead-end of sorts. A plain white building sat in a clearing on the left. Large green lettering painted on the broad pitched roof couldn't be missed, identifying it as the correct location. The structure resembled a warehouse with a string of rectangular windows set high along the side. Other buildings of varying sizes stood at a distance, structures I assumed sheltered farm tools and equipment.

I turned in and parked next to two white pickup trucks on the asphalt pad by the main building. The Grimes Corporation logo on the truck doors identified ownership. While getting out of the Explorer, I noticed two Quonset hut hangars a hundred yards or so to the left of the main building. An adjacent airstrip had an east-west alignment. I surmised that one of the hangars held the remains of Tony Grimes' wrecked plane.

I pulled open the only entry door I saw and stepped into a room, hardly more than twelve-by-twelve in size. It was furnished with a desk and a couple of chairs. No one was present.

I was about to knock on an interior door, when the rumbling sound of muted male voices came from the other side of it. As the volume of the exchange increased, I stood there feeling like an eavesdropper. Within seconds, they launched into an outright shouting match, loud enough to recognize that one of them was older than the other, the older man saying, "He's dead, Fillmore. Things will be different now."

Abruptly, the door burst open and a man, his face flushed with anger, bolted past me and slammed out the exterior door I'd entered. It's a good thing I'm light on my feet. If I hadn't stepped out of the way, he'd have flattened me.

CHAPTER 7

Aside from his florid face, the only part of his appearance I caught as he left, was his square jaw, thinning hair and glasses.

Just as abruptly, a younger man pushed through the interior doorway. He halted when he saw me. Startled, his face flushed. With a couple seconds hesitation, he ran his hand over the back of his head in a self-conscious gesture. "I'm sorry you had to witness that. You must be Deena Powers."

"That's me." I reached in my purse for my license and displayed it as proof while I took his measure. He was about five-ten, trim and muscled. Age, late thirties. His features were rather ordinary except for intense blue eyes. He had dark cropped hair and wore the currently-popular shadow of a beard. His attire was simple: blue jeans, tan tee-shirt & sneakers.

He gave my license a glance before displaying a forced smile. "Fillmore Grimes," he said. "The man who just left is my Uncle Willie. My father's death has everyone on edge, and Uncle Willie's not making it any easier. It's unfortunate, but he's got quite a temper. He's acting like he should be in charge now that he's the oldest male in the family. He manages the financial side of the business, but it takes more than a head for numbers to run an outfit like this one. It's more about managing crops and people."

With a brief grimace, he glanced at the floor, then back at me. "But that's not what you are here to learn. Let me get the envelope I prepared for you. It's on my desk." He went back through the door, reappeared in a moment and handed me a manila envelope with my name printed on the side. "This is the information you'll need. If there's anything else...."

I opened the end and extracted a single page, a letter authorizing me to search the county tax rolls for the property described by the parcel number listed. "It's a start," I said. "Claudine said you could fill me in on the history of the property."

He gave a quick chuckle. "According to family lore, Dad's great-grandfather Fillmore Grimes, the one I'm named for, won that parcel of land in a card game sometime in the late 1860s. He came to California thinking to get rich, but by the time he arrived the best gold claims were all spoken for. He decided the real gold might be in growing wheat." He scratched the lobe of his ear and grinned. "But when he went to look at his prize, half of it was under water. The poor sap had been swindled." Fillmore laughed outright. "The shoreline of Tule Lake, as it was called then, varied depending on the amount of rainfall. It had been a wet winter that year."

"Did he record his ownership?"

A brief shrug. "I don't know just when the deed was recorded. It would have been difficult to have it surveyed when it was under water, but I imagine one of our ancestors had it done. Claudine knows the details of our lineage. You'll have to talk to her for exact names. According to what I've heard, my grandfather used to say that after the lake receded, a farmer could get a good crop of winter wheat if the weather was right."

"Can you give me directions to the property? I'd like to have a look at it."

He grinned. "I can do better than that. I'll fly you out there. It's not far. You can see it better from the air."

"It sure would save me some time. Thanks."

Fillmore opened the outer door. "Come on. We'll take my truck over to the hangar."

I followed him out, then held up the envelope. "I'll just put this in my car." I deposited it on the seat and locked up, then turned to climb into the cab of his pickup, a model that likely cost forty-grand.

As we pulled away, I glanced at the old Explorer and wondered when I'd feel rich enough to buy a new one. We'd earmarked most of the proceeds from selling the property in Ortega Bay to a college fund for Peggy Lou's education.

A moment later he pulled up next to the closest hangar. We climbed out and walked around to the big doors. He fiddled with a paddle lock, and soon the hinges squawked as he swung the doors open. Inside stood a plane that looked identical to the one his father had been flying when it crashed.

"Wait here," Fillmore said. "I'll roll it out and then help you get in." He stepped inside the building and reappeared with a long-handled hook he attached above the front wheel of the plane. I was a little surprised to see how he easily pulled it out into the open. He walked around the plane, checking various parts of the exterior. When he mounted the wing on the far side and opened the door he called to me. "Walk around the tail."

I did as he instructed, and after opening the cockpit, he reached out his hand to help me climb onto the wing. He slid into the pilot seat, and I followed, settling down on the passenger side. He reached across me to secure the door.

After flipping a lever, the instrument panel lit up, rapidly changing colors. A second later the engine buzzed to life, and we moved toward the tarmac, coming to a stop at the edge of the asphalt strip. I looked back at the other hangar, again wondering about the location of the wreckage.

I guess he noticed, because he said, "I suppose you're curious about Dad's plane. The authorities have it sealed in the other hangar until the NTSB gets around to the final inspection. I'm not sure when that will be. Soon, I hope." He put on a headset and handed a second one to me. "Put this on so you can hear me."

With that, he muttered something into his mic, and then guided the plane out onto the runway with the nose pointing west. The sound of the engine increased to a roar, then moved forward and we lifted off.

"How long have you been flying?" I asked after adjusting the earphones and mic.

One corner of his mouth turned up in a half-smile, and he gave me a side-glance, perhaps bemused, thinking I didn't trust his skill. "Since I was a teenager. This is my third plane. The first was a little Piper Cherokee. Loved that plane. The first thing Dad told me about flying was, 'Don't get over-confident. Flying is a risk, a calculated risk, but keep in mind, there are no old, bold pilots.'"

I had to think a second to decipher the meaning.

He shrugged. "It's just an old adage." He rattled off the plane's vital specs, most of which were lost on me. I was busy watching landmarks below shrink in size, but I don't think he noticed. He'd barely finished his recitation when he tilted the left wing downward and pointed to a field below. A plow was working its way across it, leaving a plume of dust in its wake. I gazed at the expanse. It was hard to imagine the area had once been covered by a vast inland lake. It had been there for hundreds of years, but was totally gone. I wondered if it were possible that the next hundred years would turn the entire valley into a desert.

"This is it, and over there is the well," he said, pointing to the southeast corner of the field below. Guiding the plane in a circle just outside the perimeter, he continued. "Originally it was a whole section, but one of the ancestors sold off quarter-sections to buy other parcels further north, including the land where the headquarters is located."

"What powers the pump?" I asked as I rubber-necked for a better look.

"A gasoline engine. You can see it standing right next to it."

"How far is it from your headquarters?"

"By ground? About eighteen miles."

"Have you met Casitas Brown?"

His brow pinched together. "No, and I hope I never do. Cliff Jessup is handling the case for us."

As we headed back north, he pointed to a field below us just ahead. "See that dark spot? That's where Dad crashed."

I raised up in my seat to see. He tilted the plane sharply, making my stomach do a flip-flop. I had to look quick, but saw where the plane had plowed through whatever crop was planted there before coming to a stop. I nodded and sunk back into place.

Nothing more was said during our return to the airfield. As we approached, the green lettering on the roof of the main building stood out. Anyone flying over would easily know their location, and I supposed that was the purpose.

The landing was smooth. He taxied to a stop by the hangar. I was about to pull off the headset when he turned to me. "I find it hard to believe the accident was pilot error. Dad was the most exacting man I know. He drilled me over and over about the importance of pre-flight checks and the annual inspection." The crease in his brow deepened, his pain evident.

"It must be torture waiting to find out what happened," I said. "I'm so sorry."

I removed the headset and handed it to him, opened the door and hoisted myself out onto the wing. He followed and lent a hand, so I could safely jump to the ground.

"Who does your mechanical work on the planes?" I asked as he stepped down.

"Mike Horn. He has a place up in Gateway for the FAA inspections. He's been doing them for as long as I can remember. And not just ours. He did the maintenance on Aunt Vivian's plane too. She learned to fly about the same time as Dad, but then sold her plane after her husband, Uncle Lennie, died." He motioned toward the nose of the plane.

I waited by his truck while he stowed it in the hangar, and we drove back to the office in silence. As we pulled up to park, his cell phone rang. I got out and stood by my car, waiting to say goodbye.

He snaked the phone out of his back pocket and tapped the face of it as he responded to the call. "I don't know," he said into the phone. A pause and he took a deep breath. "Yes, you're right. I forgot it's your birthday. I'll be there by seven."

Fillmore stepped out of the truck and walked around to where I stood. "It's not good to forget a woman's birthday," he said with a sheepish grin. "I better get into town and do some shopping."

"Your mistake was to admit it." I smiled and stuck out my hand. "Thanks for the ride." I climbed into my SUV, turned the key and backed out.

On the drive back to town, I considered his doubts about the crash and those of Claudine's. It was probably part of the grieving process, but it sure made me curious about what the investigators would report and how the family would react.

CHAPTER 8

Since Tuesday happened to be the day Madge and Wilbur were scheduled to visit Golden Hills Care Home, I had to pick up Peggy Lou from nursery school. I arrived just as the kids began pouring out of the building and into the fenced area in front. They were waving drawings made that morning. Most parents cheerfully praised the offerings, although I heard one woman shout, "Hurry up. Get in, get in. I haven't got all day."

I dodged a couple of kids barreling through the gate and met Peggy Lou. She held up the painting she'd made. I took it, held it at arm's length, and focused on two brown stick figures. Since they had four legs, I deduced they were supposed to be dogs.

"You made a picture of Jeff and Wilbur," I said with enthusiasm. She grinned. I'd guessed correctly. I took her hand to lead her to the SUV. Mrs. Hughes, her teacher, a tall, angular woman in a flowered smock, hurried to cut me off. "Mrs. Walker. Oh, Mrs. Walker, I'm afraid I have some distressing news." She reached out as though she might grab my shoulder, but didn't. "Peggy Lou bit another child today."

I reared back. "Gosh. I'm so sorry." I glanced at my daughter. She was looking down at her shoes.

"Such behavior is unacceptable," the teacher continued. "You must stress to her how important it is that we learn to get along with others."

She yammered on about the value of early childhood education and how it prepared for life, but I wasn't listening. I was having an instant recall of my own nursery school days. Especially the day I almost bit a chunk out of Randy Smith's hand when he tried to knock over my sand castle for the third time.

Breaking out of my reverie, I assured her I'd have a talk with my child.

"Thank you," she said. With a sweet smile, she leaned over and spoke to Peggy Lou. "We're going to have a better day tomorrow, aren't we?"

I led Peggy to the SUV, helped her into her car seat and snapped the buckles. "Can we go see Wilbur?" she asked.

"We have something to talk about." I closed the door and went around to the driver's side, climbed in and turned in my seat. Facing my daughter, I said, "You can't bite people. They won't like you, and you won't have any friends."

Her lip quivered and her eyes filled with tears. "He... he..." She reached up and lifted a handful of her hair with a mock jerk.

"He pulled your hair?"

She nodded and wiped her nose on the back of her hand.

I had no solution for her dilemma. In my own case, I told the kid I'd gouge his eyes out with the sand shovel if he came near me again.

I shifted in the seat and started the car. "Today, you get to go to the office and see Bert. You can show her your picture, but first I need to stop for some gasoline."

A couple of blocks south of the nursery school was Avila's Quick Mart. I used my credit card, and as soon as the tank was full, pulled across the street to Casey's drive-in to order some lunch for us. With enough grilled cheese sandwiches and fries for three, plus a carton of milk, I pointed the Explorer in the direction of the office.

Patrons of the doughnut shop next door often use our parking spaces, an inconvenience for us. But by noon when I returned, the lot was clear. I juggled the lunch bags as I unbuckled Peggy Lou from her car seat. She hopped to the pavement and reached up her hand, wanting to carry her own sack. When we were inside, Bert exhibited delight over Peggy's picture, asking questions, encouraging her to elaborate on each aspect of the painting.

When the conversation had run its course, I led Peggy in the direction of her special corner of the room. I'd purchased a child's chair and table at a yard sale, gave it a paint job and fashioned a place with a rug for her to occupy herself when she visited the office. Bert had added a kid-sized bookcase for books and toys from home. Peggy Lou had been quick to take ownership of the space.

I spread out a napkin in front of her and placed a cheese sandwich & fries on it, then opened the carton of milk and stuck in the straw. Content she could manage the simple meal, I fished a couple of sodas from our under-counter fridge for Bert and I, and we turned our attention to our part of the lunch while I recounted the morning's flying adventure.

When lunch cleanup was finished, I provided my daughter with scratch paper, so that she could expand her drawing talent. Since I didn't have anything for Bert to do, she left, saying she planned to sign up at the local gym.

I turned my attention to the computer. My knowledge of county history was sparse, mainly what I'd learned from Aunt Madge in general conversation. If I'd been exposed to it during the year I attended Four Creeks High, I sure didn't remember much. I was grateful the internet could help make up for my deficiency.

A database of historical state maps proved useful. I scrolled through the list to find Delta County. The description of each included the year of origin, the map maker and the current repository. Two in particular caught my attention. The first was a framed map dated

1867, showing the railroad lines, townships, plus school and election districts. According to the legend, it just happened to be hanging on the wall in the history room at the library in Delta.

Since 1867 was about the time the original Fillmore Grimes had immigrated to this county, I decided visiting the library might be useful. The other one was from 1892 and included local cities, school houses, churches, canals, vineyards and roads. It was stored in the same room at the library. I jotted down the pertinent reference numbers.

On another site, I came across a photo of a color drawing of the lake's shoreline in various years. The lake had receded sufficiently by 1875 to make the area where Grimes owned land free of surface water. In other words, he could have farmed it by that time. I hit the print command.

I typed Delta County early deeds into the search engine and turned up a promising database, but it turned out to be disappointing. The earliest records it held were in 1949. I was going to have to do my job the old-fashioned way, search the courthouse records as the clerk had insisted.

By the time Peggy Lou and I reached home late that afternoon, a fast-moving storm had swept across the valley and bunched dark clouds against the Sierras.

Rain pelted us as I made a dash for the house from the SUV with Peggy clinging to me like a little monkey. I put her down on her feet when we reached the shelter over the door to the kitchen. I was fumbling to unlock the door when lightning flashed, followed by a boom of thunder that sounded so close I wondered if the next strike might hit the tall pine in the front yard.

As soon as I pushed our way inside, Peggy ducked under the kitchen table and covered her ears. I felt inclined to do the same, but thought I should act like a grown-up. Through the windows in the living room, I saw the horses down in the pasture acting skitterish, flesh quivering. It occurred to me that one of them might attempt to jump the fence. But there was nothing I could do. If Buzz had been home, he would have gone out to try to calm them. Not me. I was almost as afraid of the horses as I was of the lightning.

Peggy started whimpering. I coaxed her out from under the table and took her to Buzz's easy chair. My poor baby. I sat, pulled her into my lap and folded my arms around her. There are some situations a parent can't do much about, except offer comfort.

The rain pounded on the roof while the thunder rolled as the storm moved east. In fifteen minutes, it had passed, leaving only jangled nerves.

We heard Buzz's pickup coming up the driveway.

"Daddy!"

Peggy climbed out of my lap, ran to the back door, twisting the knob in an attempt to open it for him.

A minute later, he stepped in and scooped her off the floor. She clung to him, babbling about the storm. "It went boom, boom."

He looked at me over her shoulder, his eyebrows raised.

"She was frightened by the thunder and lightning."

"Well, it's all over now," he said. He twirled her around and tickled her ribs. She giggled, her fear soon forgotten.

Later that evening, after Peggy Lou had been tucked into bed, Buzz and I relaxed in the living room. I silenced the TV and related the sad fact that his daughter had bit another child at school.

He chuckled. "I admit it's not the best way to deal with conflict, but I doubt she'll be a menace to society. Relax. You're a good mom and she'll grow up to be just like you."

I decided not to tell him about my own sandbox war, or about the time I blew a fuse and beaned my badminton opponent with the racket when we disagreed about the rules of the game. She was so stubborn, I'd felt it was justified, but I had a hard time finding a partner after that.

CHAPTER 9

It rained during the night and was still sprinkling when I pulled into the office parking lot after dropping Peggy Lou off at nursery school. April showers are supposed to bring May flowers, but I was in no mood to be optimistic. Buck Harper's ugly mug had invaded my dreams the night before, and I wanted to know he was back behind bars. It had been well over twenty-four hours since his escape. In hopes Judy Amrine had heard some news, I decided to call her as soon as I got inside.

I made a dash for the sheltered walkway that ran along the front of the building, unlocked the door and turned off the alarm. After laying my handbag on my desk, I shrugged out of my damp jacket and hung it on the antique coat rack I'd found at a yard sale. I sat down at my desk and tapped her number into the phone pad.

"I hope I didn't call too early," I said when she answered.

"Nope. I was just about to leave for my exercise class."

"I don't want to make you late, but has there been any word on Harper?"

"They haven't caught him, if that's what you mean. His picture was on the news this morning, but no one has seen him since the highway incident."

"What highway incident?"

"In El Centro. The cops weren't sure who it was at first. A liquor store was robbed. The police were quick to get there, and one of them even got off a shot at him, but didn't think he was hit. He escaped into an industrial area. I guess the clerk gave a good description even after Harper cracked his head. Later in the night, the news reported, he stole a car. They chased him down the 86 till he crashed it and took off into some bushes. They actually closed down the highway for several hours to hunt for him. He got away again."

"Wonder where he got the gun. Are they certain it was Harper ?"

"Well, not a positive ID, but they're sure acting like it. 'Believed to be,' is how it was worded this morning."

"Damn. Keep me posted, will you?"

"Sure. Has he got you spooked? Don't worry. I'll call the minute I hear they catch him. But gotta go."

"Thanks." I clicked off, and with a sigh, put the phone back on its stand. El Centro was at least 400 miles away, I reasoned. As bad as Judy's report sounded, the fact that Harper hadn't been apprehended yet didn't mean he was a threat to anyone in Four

Creeks. I wondered if he would still have contacts around Ortega Bay, someone who'd take him in. He was originally from that area. I imagined he needed money. Would he contact his half-sister? It didn't seem likely.

I got up and went to our kitchenette. Barely focusing on what I was doing, I filled the coffee pot and pressed the start button. It's a good thing the phone started ringing. Everything I'd been thinking was sheer speculation and only served as a distraction. I had better things to do. I went to my desk and picked up the receiver.

The caller was Leon Phillips, owner of the local hardware store, and the husband of one of Aunt Madge's friends from the Women of Colonial Heritage. Business was good, he said, and he had the names of a couple of people he wanted vetted, possible new employees.

It was the type of assignment any investigator would be happy to have: a few phone calls, a computer search and a report. In most cases, it would take only a few hours, and best of all, it was something Bert was experienced enough to handle. I described my fee structure, and he agreed. As soon as I scribbled down the information, the call ended. I pulled a contract out of my file drawer, filled in the blanks and was just sealing it in an envelope when Bert came in the front door.

"Coffee smells good," she said as she ambled over to hang her coat next to mine. She was wearing black knee-high boots with snug purple pants tucked in. A loose floral shirt topped off her ensemble.

I laid the information and envelope about the case on her desk and went back to our mini-bar. Taking down a jar of creamer, a container of sugar packets, plus two mugs from the cabinet shelf, I set them on the counter, then poured the coffee for each of us.

Bert joined me. "Thanks." She loaded her mug with sugar and creamer, stirred and studied my face. "You look as gloomy as the sky outside."

"The police haven't caught up with that fugitive." I took a gulp of coffee before continuing. "And apparently he was spotted down in El Centro, but not apprehended. He's such a violent creature, everyone will be better off when he's back in prison."

I pointed to her desk. "Be a peach and take that down to the hardware store and get Mr. Phillips' signature on it. He's good for the money." I swallowed another gulp and set the cup aside. "I need to go talk to Claudine Morales before I go to the courthouse to search old land records."

Bert took her coffee to her desk, picked up the envelope and glanced at the notes I'd made. "Sure. Maybe I'll walk. It's about quit raining. I'll get started on the background checks too."

"Thanks."

I grabbed my jacket, retrieved my handbag and started for the door, leaving Bert studying the details on the paper.

Fifteen minutes later, I guided the Explorer into a parking space in front of Claudine's store-front gallery. The location, wedged between a gift shop and a nail salon, was in a strip mall just off the main highway that bisected the city of Delta. Rust-colored, bouffant-style awnings shaded the windows and each had enormous posters plastered at odd angles. They invited visitors to return for the gala exhibition the coming Saturday evening.

I got out of the SUV, went to the entrance and rapped on the glass. A moment passed before Claudine appeared, unlocked the door and escorted me inside. She was wearing blue culottes and a loose-fitting, pink cotton shirt with long sleeves. Her blonde hair was tied back in a ponytail.

"My brother told me you arrived at the office in time to witness one of Uncle Will's tantrums. I'm so sorry about that. He's really a sweet guy most of the time."

I shrugged. "Your family's been under a great deal of stress. Disagreements are bound to occur."

I glanced around. It was a cavernous room, something that hadn't registered the day I'd been focused on the painting of the little girl and her dog.

The walls were almost bare with only a few paintings displayed, a stark change from the day I'd been a customer. A half-dozen easels stood empty, awaiting an assigned occupant. In the center of the room, a long table draped with a gold-colored cloth awaited the all-important refreshments.

Claudine motioned for me to follow and led me over to where a dark-haired woman was arranging four-foot, fake bird of paradise stalks in a urn.

"I want you to meet my friend, Roz Chambers," Claudine said as we approached.

The woman turned with a broad smile, showing a perfect line of teeth. They must have cost her a fortune in dental work. She was dressed in denims and a blue plaid shirt with the sleeves rolled up. She nodded and stuck out her hand which I accepted.

"This is Deena Powers," Claudine continued, "just in case you ever need a private investigator again. She's doing some work for the family business."

"I could have used your talent four years ago when I couldn't find my husband's secret bank accounts," Roz said.

I pulled my business card from my purse and handed it to her. "Just in case," I said, smiling.

"Roz took the day off to help me out," Claudine said. "She works in the D. A.'s office. I'm in such a state of jitters, I must apologize. Most of the paintings haven't arrived, and the caterer tells me he can't have the refreshments here until after six o'clock. I'm not sure he can get everything set up before people start arriving."

She indicated a desk on the other side of the room. It looked like it had been strategically located so someone could watch to see that nothing was spirited out of the building.

"I brought a copy of our family tree my mother made years ago," she said as she ushered me over to the desk. "It should contain the information you require." She pulled out a chair. "Have a seat."

I fished a notebook and pen out of my purse. "I thought it best to have an accurate list of your family names to avoid possible confusion. Especially your grandfather's full, legal name. I may need to work backward from the present day."

She picked up a large manila envelope, extracted a nine-by-eleven sheet of paper, and smoothed it out on the desk's surface. "My grandfather was Walt Grimes, actually Walter. He died when I was five, but I remember him."

"Grandpa Powers was a great guy," I said with a smile. "Taught me how to fish." I focused on the carefully printed names.

"I wish I could say that about *my* grandfather. He was a hard man, narrow-minded and cruel in some ways."

I looked up from the sheet of paper, startled by the harshness in her tone.

"Uncle Will was born with a malformed foot. My mother told me my grandfather blamed Grandma for the deformity. It didn't matter to him that the doctors were able to straighten the foot so that Uncle Will was able to walk perfectly fine. He could never live up to Grandfather Walt's standards. Before he passed on, he groomed my dad to take over the farming business, and left instructions in his will to look after Uncle Will like he was some kind of feeble-minded child." She took a deep breath. "I'm sorry. More than you wanted to know. I didn't mean to get off track. I know you need to get going."

"After I locate the original record, the next step will be to hire a surveyor."

"I'll leave that to Fillie. He can contact my husband. I'm sure he already knows of one."

"Can I ask why you didn't ask your husband to find the old deed to the property? He could have done it without incurring the expense. Not that I mind having the money, I assure you."

Claudine gave out a puff. "He thinks he's a wheeler-dealer real estate agent, too important to take time for such a task. He says the housing boom going on right now is not going to last, and he's got to make all the money he can. It's his opinion that we should sell the land you're researching to a developer friend of his, argues that it's not efficient to have a crop so far from our other farms. He's been talking to Dad, trying to convince him. But Dad told him he'd never give it up. It's been in the family forever. I think Fillie was more sympathetic to the idea."

Musical notes emanated from a gray purse resting on a chair near the table. She reached inside, pulled out a cell phone and looked at it. "It's Fillie. Excuse me." She lifted the phone to her ear.

I turned my attention to the family tree. It was the standard configuration I was familiar with due to Aunt Madge's association with the Women of Colonial Heritage. Madge still held the office of Registrar even though the organization had shrunk since the murder of one of the members a few years ago. I jotted a list of the names from successive generations on my notepad.

"Sheriffs' cars? What for?" Claudine said into the phone.

I glanced up.

She listened with an expression of puzzlement, then put her hand to her chest. "I can't leave here, not now."

The voice at the other end grew loud enough for me to hear, though I couldn't distinguish the words.

"I just can't, Fillmore. I'm responsible for other people's property. There's a delivery truck full of valuable paintings due any minute. When it arrives, I have to go over the inventory and make sure every painting is labeled properly."

She turned to me. "Could you go out to the headquarters and find out what's going on? He says the NTSB people are back with some others from the Sheriff's Department. He says they've strung yellow tape around the hangar and won't tell him anything. I can't leave here until the security guard arrives at five o'clock."

It wasn't part of my plan for the day, but the news of yellow tape could mean only one thing. A pack of wild dogs couldn't have kept me away.

CHAPTER 10

Thirty minutes later, I turned onto the drive leading to the Grimes Corporation headquarters. I slowed as I approached the office parking lot. Sure enough, like a scene from one of those crime dramas on TV, yellow crime scene tape was strung around the hangar and attached to tree trunks nearby. An SUV with a state license plate was parked in the shade near the hangar door, and two sheriffs' cars sat off to one side. Three uniformed men stood at the entrance watching activities going on inside the building.

As I parked and got out of the car, I scanned the group for Fillmore Grimes. Not seeing him, I headed for the office door, but hesitated when my attention was drawn to the profile of a young woman around the corner, leaning against the side of the building. She was holding a wad of tissues to her nose. Little shudders her shoulders made indicated she was crying. I made a guess that she worked for the corporation, and curious, ambled in her direction. As I approached, I noticed her youth, not much more than a teenager. Her thin arms protruded from a short-sleeved green dress, a light fabric, perhaps a cotton and polyester blend. It was belted around a small waist.

Not wanting to startle her, I said "Excuse me." She startled anyway and turned with a jerk. Her short black hair and brown eyes made me think of the actress, Ann Hathaway.

"I'm sorry," I said, "but I was wondering where I might find Fillmore Grimes." I admit, it was a ploy.

She said nothing, but waved a hand toward the building behind her.

Moving closer, I said, "You seem very upset."

She nodded, and wiped her nose. "It's old Mr. Grimes. I overheard them say they think his plane was tampered . . ." She drew a sharp breath and sniffed into the tissues.

"Did they say how?"

She shook her head, removing the tissue from her face. "Just that there'll be an investigation. I don't know what to do."

I reached out and touched her shoulder. "There's nothing *for* you to do."

"They're going to ask me a lot of questions, I just know it." She straightened and blew her nose.

"My name's Deena Powers. What's yours?"

"Holly. I'm the receptionist here."

"Well, Holly. Just answer the questions truthfully. It'll be okay."

"You don't understand."

When someone says that, you can bet there's more to the story. I felt like a cat with my paw in a fish bowl. What did this girl know? "Did you see anyone out by the hangar the day of the crash?"

She shook her head again. "I heard them argue," she whispered.

I had to lean close to hear her. "Who?" I asked, careful not to raise my voice.

She glanced at me sideways. Again, a whisper. "Old Mr. Grimes and his brother."

"What did they argue about?"

"Money. I didn't want to hear them. I went into the bathroom and shut the door, but I heard anyway."

Clearly, this girl thought she'd been a witness to something important. "Holly, did you hear everything that was said?"

She looked up at me with pleading eyes. "Yes, but I don't remember it all. They were shouting. I didn't *want* to hear it. I put my hands over my ears."

A man's voice came from back by the office door, "Holly!"

She jerked to attention, and dashed out into the open. "Yes, sir."

"What are you doing? Get in here and take care of this phone."

She glanced back at me, and then hurried away.

I remained still, mulling over what I'd just heard. Holly had witnessed an argument she thought was about money. Money, the great motivator. Poor kid. Loyalty versus the law.

Over by the hangar, the men stood with their hands in their pockets, a stance I interpreted as boredom. I let my gaze wander, speculating about how someone might approach the hangar unseen. Other than several farm equipment buildings, the area was open.

Off to my right, some distance away, maybe three hundred yards or a little more, stood an older, two-story Craftsman home with a classic front porch. Its green wood siding made it blend in with ancient trees surrounding it. Someone had added a modern garage in the back and a driveway that led off to the main road. Whoever lived there would have had a good view of both hangars and the surrounding area. If evidence proved the aircraft had, indeed, been tampered with, the authorities would soon be knocking on that door.

I took a deep breath. Time to go talk to Fillmore Grimes. I moved back to the main entrance to the office building, pulled open the door and stepped inside. Holly's head jerked up from behind the laptop computer, her eyes wide, as though surprised I was still around.

"I'm here to see Fillmore Grimes," I said, smiling. "He's expecting me." I fished a couple of my business cards out of my purse and laid them on the desk where she sat. She picked up one and gazed at it. A tiny gasp escaped her lips when my profession registered. She glanced up at my face, concern in her eyes. I could see her thoughts churning. Would I give away her secret?

She rose and went through the inner door. A minute later, she returned. "First door on the right," she said, and held the door open for me.

I stepped into a wide hall. A skylight provided light from above. Doors on either side meant additional offices. The passageway continued to the far end of the building, terminating in a bright open room and another door to the outside.

With a quick knock on the door Holly had indicated, I entered Fillmore Grimes' office. He was seated behind his desk, leaning over, stuffing a thick batch of papers into an upright briefcase positioned next to his knee. Cardboard boxes of various sizes sat by the file cabinets, each full of manila folders or other office items.

He snapped the case shut, straightened, and greeted me by motioning to a visitor's chair. "Take a seat." He leaned his arms on the desk's surface. "I was hoping my sister would change her mind."

I settled onto the chair. "She wanted to, but asked me to come and report back to her."

"You can see what's happening. They've decided there's something suspicious about the condition of the cables that controlled my father's plane, that they might have been tampered with." He rubbed his temple with his index finger. "I think they're wrong."

"Who informed you?"

"It wasn't until after I phoned Claudine. One of the men from the NTSB, the one with the big paunch. About an hour after they arrived, he came over and said when they were going over the photos, they thought the cables looked like there was more damage than routine wear. They decided to have another look at them in person. They're going to cut out segments to send to their lab for microscopic examination. It's crazy." He paused, and his eyebrows pulled together. "I had an appointment to see the insurance underwriter about filing a claim. I was just about to leave when the investigators arrived. I had to cancel it."

He pulled open the lower desk drawer and lifted out a bottle of Crown Royal and two glasses. Twisting the cap off the whiskey, he poured a generous measure into one of the glasses, then raised the bottle and nodded an invitation to me.

I held up my hand. "No thanks. A bit too early for me."

"On a day like this, the clock be damned." With that, he lifted the glass and downed the contents with one gulp.

I motioned to the boxes on the floor. "Are you moving?"

He laughed and poured more liquor into his glass. "I'm taking over my dad's office before Uncle Willie has a chance to move his stuff into it. He thinks he's

going to be head honcho, but I've got news for him."
His expression changed, became more serious. "This is
a family corporation. Dad was President and CEO. I'm
Vice President with Claudine as Corporation Secretary,
and then Uncle Willy as CFO. Spouses are included and
descendents have voting rights once they reach age
twenty-one. It's all filed with the California Secretary
of State.

"With Dad gone, I'm next in line." He took a
swallow from the glass. "There's a board meeting
scheduled for Monday. I know I can count on Claudine.
I suppose Aunt Vivian will side with Uncle Willie. He's
always been her favorite." He finished what was left in
the glass, set it down on the desk and capped the bottle.
"Unless you want to help me move all these boxes..."
He gave me a crooked grin and pushed back his chair.

I shook my head and rose, ready to leave.

"Then tell Claudine I'm don't know when we'll
hear what that tribe out there has to say. I'll call her
tonight." He stood and reached for the bottle. "Hey,
maybe that Casitas Brown bitch sneaked in here and
sabotaged those cables in Dad's plane. Whadaya
think?"

I stifled a laugh and opened the door. "So long, Mr.
Grimes."

"Hey, call me Fill."

Back in the reception area, I smiled at Holly and pointed my thumb in the direction of the inner door. "I think your boss needs some help."

CHAPTER 11

I stepped out into the open air in time to see two people standing in front of a TV news van parked not far from the taped-off area. The man had a commercial video camera propped on his shoulder. It looked like he was recording the scene. Next to him a woman stood with a microphone in her hand. How'd they hear about the new development? A police scanner, no doubt.

The woman moved in front of the camera, and that's when I recognized her. Walking toward them, I realized how little her appearance had changed in twenty-some years. Her hair color was the same, same style, and she'd kept her athletic figure. Robin Masters had been a cheerleader at Four Creeks High back when I attended there. She'd been a pain in the butt then, and I figured she'd be the same now. A loud mouth, she'd been one of the main gossip-mongers on campus. And to top it off, she had her sights set on Buzz Walker when he started dating me. As I approached, a few of the lies she'd spread about me bubbled out of my memory banks.

I marched up and stood right next to the camera man, pulled my license out of my purse and held it up at her eye level. She stopped her comments to the camera and motioned to him.

"This is private property," I said.

She focused on my license for a second. Then her jaw dropped. "Oh my God. If it isn't Deena Powers. Where'd *you* come from?" She nodded to the camera man. "It's okay, Sam. We probably got about all we can for now."

"I represent the Grimes Corporation," I said, returning my license to my purse. "You should leave."

"Come on, Deena. Let bygones, be bygones. I know. I acted like a shithead back at Four Creeks High. I'm sorry. How about I buy you lunch?" She stepped forward and held out her hand. It was like watching a cobra coil.

I admit it, old grudges die hard, and I wasn't about to let this opportunity pass. "Unless you're anxious to have a trespassing charge filed against you," I turned and directed my attention to the camera man, "you'd better erase that recording."

His eyes narrowed, but he gave me a grudging nod and moved toward the van, leaving Robin muttering under her breath.

After they were tucked inside and on their way, I allowed myself a smirk. It might not last, but for the moment, clipping her wings felt good.

I was still smiling when I climbed into the Explorer, ready to turn the key and prepare for the return trip to Four Creeks. But before leaving, I pulled my cell phone from my purse and called Claudine. After telling her what little I knew about the investigation, and that her brother would contact her later, I backed out of the parking space.

The two-lane road leading away from the Grimes Corporation driveway had more than the usual amount of pot holes, probably from heavy farm equipment that travelled along it. I took my time, dodged the ruts, and before long pulled up to the stop sign at the main road. Another four miles and I turned north.

With a twenty-minute drive ahead of me, I flicked on the radio and was humming along with Garth Brooks when I noticed a white pickup rapidly approaching behind me. I checked my speedometer. I was travelling at the speed limit with a long s-curve ahead. Though I tensed like a cat in a dog pound, I told myself it wasn't logical to think Buck Harper was in that truck.

As the road curved to the left, I edged over to the right, a signal for him to pass. He didn't. He pulled up close behind, too close, it seemed to me—riding my tail. Annoyance shot up the back of my neck. Damn fool. With a death grip on the steering wheel, I kept glancing from the road ahead, to my rear view mirror and back again. I could see the driver's head. A baseball cap shaded his face. I braced myself, wondering if he intended to rear-end me. If that happened, his purpose would be obvious.

By the time I entered a straight stretch, my mouth was dry, and my heart pounding like an astronaut on lift-off. Suddenly, the pickup backed off and shot around me, zooming ahead, picking up speed. In less than half a minute, he was a mile down the road, soon to meet his maker in my opinion.

Relief flooded. I gripped the steering wheel to keep my sweaty hands from shaking. The incident hadn't lasted more than a few minutes, but with the old memories, it felt much longer. His white pickup had triggered the memory of when Buck Harper and Dennis Colton had teamed up, and Colton had tracked my car in a similar looking truck. I took a deep breath. Judy Amrine was right, Harper being on the loose had me spooked and I didn't like it.

When I pulled into the driveway at the office, I determined to set the whole incident aside and put things into prospective. Harper's whereabouts were unknown. My normal inclination was to *do* something. In any similar situation, I would, but in this case, there was nothing I *could* do but suck it up. I simply needed to stick to business and expect the authorities would do their job.

Inside the office, it looked like Bert had made a good start on vetting Mr. Phillips' potential employees.

She'd left a note saying she was awaiting one more report and had left for the day.

The NTSB's investigation had made me curious about aircraft cables. I shrugged out of my coat before turning on the computer. I decided I'd utilize the internet to see what I could learn. After wading through a couple of sites that wanted to sell me new airplane cables, I located an article written by a pilot who described how worn cables can go unnoticed, and that inspection was critical—if you wanted to stay alive. Fillmore hadn't mentioned when his father's plane had been serviced last. I felt certain the NTSB would have checked the plane's log. Regulations demanded accurate records of maintenance be kept up to date. It would be a double tragedy if the crash turned out to have been preventable. But then, come to think of it, most accidents are preventable.

CHAPTER 12

That evening as we finished dinner, I noticed that Buzz was behaving as if he had something on his mind. He was a little too quiet. He picked up several of the dishes from the table and carried them to the sink. I followed with a few more and started scraping remnants of food into the garbage disposal. It was normal for us to chat about the day's events while we cleared the table.

He left the room, returned with a wet washcloth and sat down in front of Peggy Lou who was still enthroned in her highchair. He carefully washed her hands and face, taking his time. It was a delaying tactic.

"Come on, big girl," he said as he lifted her from the chair. I watched him carry her into the living room and put her down in front of the TV. He stuck her favorite cartoon movie in the DVD player and turned it on. As soon as happy bunnies were prancing around the screen, he came back into the kitchen, and without a word, began putting plates in the dishwasher.

"Okay," I said, looking over at him. "What's eating you? I can tell there's something you don't want to tell me. Did you quit your job? Or get fired? No. That can't be it." A thought ignited. "Oh, crap. You had to shoot someone."

He shook his head. "We received a BOLO for Buck Harper. He's escaped from prison."

"Yes, I heard. Judy Amrine called from San Diego to tell me." I'm not sure if it was pride, or what, but I didn't want him to know that Harper could still prickle my nerves. "He's probably deep in the heart of Mexico by now."

When Buzz didn't respond to my comment, I figured he was unconvinced. "Now don't tell me you think he'll come this far north. And don't suggest I stay home in case he might still be out for revenge. I'd be safer at my office in town, especially since it's just two blocks from the police department."

He didn't say anything, but took a plate and glass from my hands and put them in the dishwasher.

"He certainly wouldn't be welcome at his sister's," I said, continuing my argument. "Besides, he must hate Hester's guts since she testified against him at his trial."

I saw a slight sideways twitch of Buzz's mouth. "That's just it, Deena. He may already be here. The local PD were notified about his escape. Then this morning, a friend of Hester McKay's called them. She said she was worried when Hester didn't answer her cell phone. They went to her house for a welfare check and found her dead on her kitchen floor."

It's a good thing I wasn't holding any glassware. I'd have dropped it. "Oh, shit!" I squawked. "You think he killed her."

"Well, not very many women hold a gun to their own head."

I stumbled to a kitchen chair and sat, my guts in a knot, my brain grappling with a picture of Hester McKay lying dead on the floor. Memories swirled, memories of my car rolling when it went off the road, the pain of learning my dad was dead, yet still not knowing what really happened and assuming it was my fault. And later, Harper's attack on Madge, kidnapping me and his effort to throw me into the river like a piece of garbage.

I bent forward, my arms folded across my stomach. And then my gaze fixed on my daughter amusing herself with her blocks. Harper would remember where Aunt Madge lived. She could be in danger. My child could be in danger.

Buzz came over and put his hand on my shoulder. "We shouldn't assume anything yet. There was some drug paraphernalia on the counter. We'll have to wait until we hear more from the coroner and the investigators, but in the meantime, I think we need to make some plans, just in case."

Neither of us slept much that night. I felt Buzz turn over a dozen times as if he was thrashing out a plan to keep us safe. For me, every time I closed my eyes, I saw Harper's face like an ugly apparition. The last time I looked at the clock on the bedside table, it was after two.

I must have drifted off, because the next thing I knew, Buzz was shaking my shoulder. "Come on, honey. We need to get an early start."

"Huh?" I squinted at the bedroom window. It was daylight and the new reality came flooding back. "Okay, okay." I fumbled with the covers, twisted myself upright and slid my feet to the floor.

Buzz left the room. Still groggy, I stood and headed to the bathroom. When I came out, showered and dressed, my nose told me he'd made coffee. I was more alert, but not much. I'm not a morning person, I might have mentioned. As soon as I appeared in the kitchen, he handed me a steaming mug. I went to sit at the kitchen table, and that's when I spotted my pistol waiting there. It was the Walther PPK I hadn't had out of the gun safe since we got married. Beside it was a box of 9mm shells and the empty magazine.

I set the cup on the table and picked up the pistol, testing its weight and remembering that there's no way to make carrying a handgun comfortable. It's a tossup. If you carry a purse with a gun pouch, the extra two pounds will soon make your shoulder sore. And if you use a shoulder holster, you feel like there's an alien under your arm, plus you have to wear a jacket to conceal it, or risk scaring the daylights out of the public.

Buzz interrupted my thoughts. "Call Madge, explain the situation to her. Ask if she can care for Peggy all day today. Until we learn more about Hester McKay's murder, I don't think we should take a chance with the nursery school—the other children."

He was right. At least for the next week, we needed to make other arrangements. I swallowed some coffee. "I better call Bert too. I'll tell her to take the day off."

He nodded at the gun. "You haven't fired it in years. I've made arrangements for you to get some practice at the firing range with an instructor I know. Like I said, just in case."

My pal, Jeff, our Doberman, came down the hall from Peggy's bedroom where he had a favorite sleeping pad. He rested his gray muzzle on my knee. As I reached for the phone, I stroked and scratched the base of his velvety ear. He tilted his head, enjoying my attention.

"Come on, boy," Buzz said. He motioned to the dog and opened the back door. "Do your business. We have work for you today."

Jeff gave me sad eyes, hung his head and reluctantly went outside.

Buzz shut the door. "We'll take him along to stay with Madge and Peggy."

"He's not a young dog anymore."

Buzz smiled. "True, but he'd know what to do if either of them were threatened."

CHAPTER 13

After the phone call to Bert, and another to let the nursery school know Peggy Lou wouldn't be attending for a few days, we pulled into Madge's gravel driveway, Buzz in his pickup and me in the Explorer with Peggy Lou in her car seat. Before the vehicles came to a full stop, Madge appeared in the doorway with Wilbur sitting next to her feet.

I got out of the SUV, opened the back door, and unbuckled my daughter. She scrambled out of the seat, and as soon as her feet touched the ground, she ran to hug Madge. I grabbed the sack containing a change of clothes for Peggy and her favorite snacks.

Buzz, dressed for work, opened the back of the SUV. Jeff jumped out, and Wilbur scampered to meet him. After the usual dog greeting of circling and sniffing, Wilbur gave Jeff's ear a nip and the two of them were off to Madge's backyard in a playful chase.

Madge smiled down at Peggy Lou, who clung to her leg, looking up at her. "Go on inside, dear. I want to talk to your parents. I think Barney is on the television."

Peggy scooted through the door, and Madge closed it behind her. She moved in our direction, her expression serious. Looking directly at Buzz, she said, "Do you really think that criminal is here in town and intends to harm us?" Her tone made the question sound like he was back in her sixth-grade class.

"I can't predict his movements, so until we know more, I believe it's better to err on the side of caution. Deena's going to the shooting range this morning to get some practice with her handgun."

Madge looked stricken, her eyes wide. She stared at the holstered pistol Buzz wore on his hip, as if it was the first time she'd noticed. She threw up her hands and shook her head. "Guns and a small child in the same house. I just don't know what to think. It's most distressing."

Both dogs came bounding back into the front yard. Wilbur pawed my pants leg, begging for attention. I picked him up and ruffled his long fur, giving his back a rub.

"We take all the precautions, Madge. If you remember, Grandpa Powers kept a shotgun, two rifles and a couple revolvers at the ranch."

"That was different," Madge said. "He needed them to eliminate rattlesnakes, or warn off a coyote. He taught your dad and I, even my mother, to shoot. All of us learned to safely handle guns. It was necessary."

"Yup. One day he got out his antique revolver to show me. He let me shoot it at a tin can. He told me his great-grandfather had once been a town sheriff in

Arizona."

Buzz interrupted. "You two can reminisce. I've got to go to work." He leaned over and kissed me on the cheek. "You know where to go. Lee Graham will be your instructor. He's expecting you."

I nodded and watched him get into his truck, back out and head down Indian Hill.

"I better get going too," I said. "I'll be back by noon to check on you two. Thanks. I'm sure you had other plans for today."

Madge smiled. "She's no trouble. I'll have some lunch ready. Be careful."

I headed south out of town, then west toward Lakeview and watched my odometer, so I wouldn't miss the turnoff to Butler Field. The weapons range had once been a 560 acre training base used to train World War II pilots. Few remnants of the wartime era buildings remained, though the old name stayed. Sold after the war, it served as a private airfield for several years, but then the Delta County Sheriff's Association acquired the field and transformed it into a modern practice range, now open to the public for a fee.

The directions Buzz had given me made the place easy to find. There was only one other vehicle in the parking lot when I pulled up in front of the building. I parked, took my pistol, full magazine & extra box of shells from the glove box and put them in my purse.

Even a few days of carrying the extra weight was going to make my shoulder ache.

I went inside the building and found myself in a spacious area with a large classroom and a small coffee shop next to the check-in desk. I paid my fee and met Lee Graham as he came in the rear door. At six feet tall, he towered over me. Clearly a man comfortable with his size, he greeted me with a broad smile and a firm hand grasp.

"Buzz said you need to brush-up on your skill with your weapon." He opened the door and ducked his head as he ushered me outside. He motioned to a counter. "Let's see what you brought."

I deposited my little arsenal. He looked at it, raised his eyebrows and nodded. "What you have here is intended for close-range. But I guess you already knew that. Let's get started."

Buzz had said Lee was a top-notch instructor and he was right. He handed me a pair of ear protectors and took me out to the range where he put me through my paces beginning with safety instruction.

Dad had been the one who taught me about guns and the rules. The first thing he said at the practice range that day was, "Bullets have no conscience. They don't care where they land. It's up to the person holding the gun to see to it they don't cause collateral damage."

Though I felt a little awkward at first, a couple of hours later, my right wrist ached, but I felt more comfortable with my weapon, as comfortable as anyone can be while imagining the silhouette on the paper target is a real human. On the other hand, with my enhanced confidence, I felt more in control of my future. And I was ready to protect my family, if it came to that.

As I reentered Four Creeks on the way back to Madge's house, my curiosity got the best of me. I swung by where Hester McKay had lived. Yellow tape draped around the house and yard was no surprise, nor the two police cars parked in front. I saw where the street had been cordoned off. But it was now open and I cruised by slowly. I wasn't the only one. Three other cars were ahead of me. Down at the end of the block, two women stood on a front porch watching the goings-on. Homicide is not a common event in Four Creeks, and by the expressions they exhibited, they were wishing everyone would go away.

I turned left at the corner, remembering the alleyway that ran behind those houses. I slowed to a crawl as I passed by and saw a van parked about half-way down. A man in white coveralls was loading a bulging sack into the rear of the vehicle, likely containing items the investigators hoped would reveal how and why Hester died.

When I came to the gas station on the next corner, I refilled my gas tank, then pulled around and followed

Main Street east. I pictured Hester on the day I'd talked to her, back when I was first trying to trace Lottie Weston's movements. Hester'd been dressed in a gray sweat suit, her frizzy blonde hair all flat on one side from lying in bed. Strange how years later the past can catch up with a person. Maybe it was due to some bad choices she'd made, or maybe the trajectory of her life had been set the day she was born into the wrong family. Either way, the result was tragic.

CHAPTER 14

True to her word, Madge had lunch ready when I arrived. She'd prepared plates of fresh garden salad sprinkled with bits of chicken. Toasted garlic bread and vanilla cookies rounded out the menu. I helped Peggy Lou climb into her high chair, the one Madge had purchased as soon as Peggy was able to sit up by herself.

With our salads in front of us, I spread my napkin and settled down to enjoy our little luncheon. Always the teacher, Madge began pointing out the different vegetables in the salad, naming them and coaching Peggy to repeat the names and test the flavors. Madge had used the same technique on me when I was a child. And, yes, like Peggy Lou, I ate foods at Madge's house I would never touch at home.

When we finished, Peggy was given a cookie, then excused to amuse herself with her coloring book.

Madge refilled our glasses of iced tea. I folded my napkin and laid it on the table. "This has been really nice, but I can't stay."

"Where are you going? Surely not to your office."

"I'm going to the courthouse in Delta to trace the origin of that property line that's being disputed."

"I don't know how you can be so cavalier with the possibility a killer may be wandering around loose."

"I've decided the scum-sucking bilge-rat is not going to control my life. I have work to do. I signed a contract with the Grimes Corporation and took their money. I'm honor-bound to live up to the contract."

Madge tilted her head, looking at me over the top of her glasses. "Very colorful, my dear. But just because you're armed, doesn't make it safe for you to be out driving around the countryside. You have a family to consider." She raised her index finger in Peggy's direction.

I nodded. "We don't really know where Buck Harper is right now. He might not be the one responsible for…" I glanced over at Peggy, "what happened to his sister. We simply have to wait and see what the investigators uncover. That could take days. Life can't come to a halt in the meantime. And for my part, if I don't have something to report by the end of next week, one of the Grimes family will likely be asking how their money is being spent."

"I would think, if you explained the situation, they'd understand." She added a spoonful of sugar to her tea and heaved a sigh. "Of course, the only one of that family I ever knew was Vivian. I thought she was a kind person."

"Vivian? Isn't she Tony Grimes' older sister?" I rose from the table and took my dishes to the sink.

"Yes. She taught special ed several years at Montgomery Elementary School while I was there. I didn't know her as well as some of the other teachers, but well enough to know she was devoted to her students."

I returned to my seat, helped myself to a second vanilla cookie and took a bite.

"One day," Madge said. "I happened to be in the teacher's room using the copy machine when Vivian came in. She was upset about a parent-teacher conference that had just concluded. She said the parents were being unreasonable, expecting her to "fix" their little girl, like a teacher was supposed to be some sort of magician. She said the child was doing her best, but the father wouldn't accept the fact that his daughter would never be as sharp as his son. The parents had left angry, and Vivian was almost in tears."

"I would think most teachers would learn not to let people like that get to them."

A furrow formed in Madge's brow. "For her, it was more personal. She said the man reminded her of her own father. Her youngest brother, Willard, had a learning disability. Besides his difficulty learning to read, there were other issues. Much to his father's displeasure, his youngest son had no interest in farming, had no aptitude for things mechanical and could *not* get the hang of shifting a tractor. For a farmer, it was unimaginable. The boy had a head for math, preferred things like chess. The result was relentless ridicule, not only from his father, but from his older brother, Tony, as well. Boys so often pattern themselves after their father. Tony had a natural mechanical ability and his father favored him.

"When Vivian realized young Will was dyslexic, she tutored him. As a result, he graduated from both high school and college. She said Will was the reason she became a teacher and wanted to teach special ed."

I shook my head. "Sounds like one of those old stories out of the Bible.

"According to her, Tony's attitude toward his younger brother didn't change even after their father's death."

"Do you still see her?"

"No. She left at the end of that school year. I heard she got a contract with one of the schools closer to where she lived." Madge stood, picked up her plate and paused, staring out the big dining room window.

I took my bag from the end of the table where I'd laid it when I came in. "Maybe you should give her a call, you know, reconnect."

Madge, roused from her reverie, twisted around and looked at me. "I guess I can't convince you."

"I'll be fine. Do you still have that baseball bat?"

She gave me a perplexed look for a second before my question registered, then said, "It's behind the door in the utility room."

"Good. Keep your cell phone handy. You have my number on speed dial, also the police. And you have the dogs." I glanced at Peggy, who was rolling a ball to Wilbur in the living room. "I'll be back about four o'clock to pick her up. I'll call if I'm going to be any later."

Peggy jumped to her feet and ran over to me. I leaned to kiss her on the cheek. "It's time for your nap, little girl."

"Can I have another cookie?"

I laughed. "You'll have to ask Aunt Madge."

Twenty minutes later, I found a parking space a block from the courthouse in Delta. I knew I wouldn't get through security with a firearm and spare magazine in my purse, so I stuck my wallet in my back pocket, took out a pen and notepad, and secured my purse in the glove box. I figured there was little risk Buck Harper would show up at a building right next door to the county jail.

I locked the Explorer, and hoofed it down the street to the entrance to join a line of people filing through the metal detector. It wasn't long before I stood in front of the building's directory next to the elevator. Not having been to the courthouse before, I didn't know where to locate the department that held the records I wanted to search.

A few people came to stand and wait for the elevator. I was only vaguely aware of a couple of men who walked up to join them, until one said, "He had his faults same as the rest of us, some good points too, I guess." The second man responded, "Maybe you can say that, but I never trusted him. He'd skin you if he had a chance; nothing illegal, but not quite ethical, either. I wouldn't be surprised if we heard someone tampered with that plane and caused it to crash."

The last statement snagged my attention. I turned to see who was speaking, but the elevator doors had opened, and they were the first to step in. I caught a glimpse of the back of a man's bald head and edged over for a better view, but the door closed before I could see inside.

The man had to have been talking about Tony Grimes. His was the only plane to have crashed recently. It gave me pause. From that man's viewpoint, some people had a low opinion of Grimes. It sort of took the shine off the impression I'd gotten the day he came to my office. After a moment's thought, I had to conclude that perhaps my judgment had been clouded by the figures written on the check he'd handed me.

CHAPTER 15

I returned my attention to the directory, located the office I was looking for and headed down the adjacent hall. By following the numbers and titles on signs above each doorway, it wasn't long before I located the Recorder's Office. I pulled the door open and was about to enter when I spotted Russell Treadwell coming out of what was likely the men's room at the end of the hall. He ran his hand over what hair he had left and moved to where two halls intersected.

Russ was an old school mate of mine at Four Creeks High as well as Aunt Madge's attorney. An attorney like Russ, with his connections, would be a good source of referrals.

I noticed he was lingering as though waiting for someone, so I let the door close and headed in his direction. I was within speaking distance when he noticed me and broke into a big smile. Though his appearance hadn't changed much from the last time I'd run into him, I did notice he was a bit more stoop-shouldered.

"Deena. How good to see you. I saw the notice in the newspaper about you opening an office in Four Creeks."

"Yes. I decided it was time to get back in the game."

"Good, good." He nodded. "How's your aunt?"

For a couple of minutes we chatted about family, then I asked, "Any chance you could send me a referral now and then?"

"You bet." He cocked his head. "Funny you should ask. A buddy of mine, a guy I play golf with, works for Central Valley Insurance. It's a subsidiary of an insurance conglomerate. His agency wrote a hefty life insurance policy for Tony Grimes. Double indemnity. I guess you heard about the plane crash."

I nodded.

"Well now," Russ went on, "he says CVI wants to be sure everything is on the up-and-up before it pays off. I could give him your card. They'll be hiring an investigator to review the accident reports and check all the details to be sure."

My heart sank. A case like that would be a real plum, open a number of doors. "Russ, that would be wonderful, except I'm already working for the Grimes Corporation on another matter."

He made a *tsk* sound. "That's too bad. It would have been a great opportunity for you."

I reached into my wallet, pulled out a few of my business cards and handed them to him. "Keep these for another time."

"Sure thing." He put them in his coat pocket and glanced at his watch. "I'm due to meet a client here in a minute."

I offered my hand. "I appreciate you thinking of me."

He grasped it and said, "No problem. We should have lunch."

"Anytime." I smiled. A busy guy like Russ rarely had free time for a casual lunch. "I better get to work myself," I said. "Good to see you."

As we went in separate directions, I wondered about the size of the insurance policy and who would benefit. Would it go to a next-of-kin, or perhaps, to pay off corporate loans?

I returned to the Records Office and went inside. A glass barrier separated a dark-haired clerk from the public. She was patiently explaining a fee structure to a woman who sounded agitated about the expense, her voice rising with each question she asked. I had to wait my turn. She finally stepped aside and reached into her handbag, so I moved to take her place.

I'd barely introduced myself to the clerk when a sound like a school fire alarm came through the public address system. Behind her, people at the many desks looked up.

"That's the notice to evacuate the building," the clerk said to me and the other woman.

Mutterings of displeasure could be heard, desk drawers opened and closed as people gathered their belongings.

The hall door opened and a uniformed security guard leaned in. "Everybody evacuate," he called out loud enough to reach the back corner of the room. He waved his arm for added emphasis, or perhaps in case someone was hearing impaired.

I grumbled under my breath and made my way to the door. Out in the hall, people were drifting toward one or the other of the main exits. Guards urged everyone to hurry along. I followed orders and soon walked out from the breeze way into a crowd. A few people strolled off to the edge of the gathering and lit up their cigarettes. Some milled around, chatting with others they knew, or making comments about the inconvenience.

I looked up toward the roof for signs of smoke, but didn't see anything to indicate there was a fire in the building. I drifted to the curb and scanned the parking lots up and down the surrounding area, though I knew it was unlikely Harper would be out there lurking behind a tree, especially with the crowd assembled behind me.

After about ten minutes, a chubby security guard in a light blue uniform appeared at the top of the paved slope that led to the entrance. "Attention," he shouted, loud enough for everyone, including God, to hear. "There's been a bomb threat. We will be doing a thorough sweep of the building. It will take at least an hour. We'll let you know when it's clear to re-enter."

As soon as he finished, I decided waiting was not a productive way to spend the Grimes Corporation's money. I'd go see what I could find in the history room at the Delta County Library. It was only a few blocks to the north. I went back to where I'd parked the SUV, got in, and maneuvered my way through a number of other drivers who'd made a similar decision.

The library building took up half a city block with a modern look to it, part brick and part stone. After locating a parking space, I dashed across the street to the entrance. The interior was cavernous and well lit with a children's wing that rivaled those found in a larger city. I inquired and was directed to a second-floor room dedicated solely to local history.

When I entered, a woman directed me to sign my name on their register, and then quickly explained the layout and listed some of the major holdings. "Now, how can I help you?"

I told her my ultimate goal, and that I was most interested in two old county maps.

She motioned to one on the wall next to the door. "I imagine this is the one you mean. But I think you might be interested in the 1892 Gazetteer also. It has the name of each land owner in a given section of land.

I'll bring it out." She went through an inner door into another room. While she was gone, I used my cell phone to take a photo of the wall map.

She soon returned with a heavy over-sized book, and placed it on a desk where I could open it and study the contents. It's numerous drawings were fascinating, and it was nearly a hour before I came across the page where I found Grimes' name neatly printed on a square of land. I pulled the tablet and pen from my purse to note the details—township 24 So., Range 24 E. The librarian was right. The book had given me information I needed.

Back in Four Creeks, I stopped at the post office to collect the mail from our P.O. box. I found three envelopes, two from utility companies, and the third, the size of a greeting card. Since my birthday wasn't until July, I didn't think it was something of that sort.

I opened the flap. It was an invitation to the Delta Art Association's exhibition to be held at Claudine's Gallery and scheduled for Saturday evening at seven-thirty. A hand-written note from Claudine apologized for the short notice, and expressed hope that I and my husband would be able to attend. I surveyed the inside of the card a second time, noting the unfamiliar names of the artists showing their work.

When I lived in Ortega Bay, I'd often gone to outdoor exhibits, especially when they were near the beach where Jeff and I frequently ran for exercise. I pondered whether I could talk Buzz into attending. Paintings and exhibitions had never been a part of our conversations. His house was decorated with western style prints, and I hadn't suggested changing it.

I picked up Peggy Lou at Madge's and headed to the ranch, where I started preparations for dinner. Buzz arrived at six-thirty, and after he'd taken care of the horses, the three of us gathered around the table.

"Did you leave Jeff with your aunt?" he asked as he snapped Peggy's highchair tray into place.

"Yes. She seems overly disturbed about the fugitive. Jeff didn't like staying behind, but Madge was pleased. She was trying to mollify him with a doggie treat as I was leaving."

Buzz eased into his seat. "Maybe we should get another dog. I still miss Butch. He was a good watchdog."

We discussed various breeds, and then I gave an account of my experience at the weapons range before I told him about the invitation to the exhibition at Claudine's gallery. As he poked around in his salad, I could tell he was trying to think of some way to get out of it. But finally, he allowed that if Madge was willing to take care of Peggy, it might be a nice change from watching old movies on TV.

"I'll ask her in the morning," I said. "How was your day?" He looked extra tired.

"I spent part of the morning trying to make peace between two homeless men who claimed the same section of the Big Oaks river bank. Each said they were there first. I finally had to run them both out. Told them they had until sundown. I'll have to go back tomorrow and see that they and all their stuff are gone.

"Then I spent the afternoon searching the neighborhood around Target trying to find a guy who snatched a woman's purse as she was getting into her car. Found her purse, but her wallet was empty. In between, it was paperwork."

"Any news related to the McKay investigation?" I asked. I glanced at Peggy to be sure she was more interested in the food on her plate than what I was saying. I've always insisted we should shield her from the seamy side of our professions as long as possible. And Buzz agreed with me.

He shook his head. "Too soon." He picked up a slice of bread from the serving basket, spread a thin layer of butter on it, and placed it on the edge of his plate. "I got to thinking about Eddie Lee, the guy she was hanging out with back when Mrs. Weston was . . . ah, snuffed. The evidence against him was pretty thin."

How well I remembered. The murder weapon, a chunk of her own fire wood, had been in the irrigation ditch too long to be useful.

Buzz's voice pulled me from the memory. "The case depended heavily on Hester's testimony, making it easier for his lawyer to get the charges watered down. I wonder if," he glanced at Peggy, "he's still living in the same place. Know what I mean?"

I put down my fork. "I sure do. And he'd have a motive." Eddie Lee had made the mistake of bragging to Hester McKay about the murder. In the end, there'd been a plea-bargain, but he still had to serve time. "Do you think he might have gotten paroled?"

"I'll see what I can find out tomorrow."

"Wouldn't the investigators be looking into that?"

Buzz rubbed the back of his hand across his chin. "Maybe not at this point. They're still working on evidence from the house. And the tox screen will take a couple of weeks."

Peggy pushed aside the pieces of broccoli on her plate. "Icky," she said and looked up at me. "What's a sum-suk'n bidge-wat?"

Buzz's eyes and eyebrows registered astonishment. "Whaaat?"

I felt heat creep up my neck and flood my face. Peggy Lou had parroted what I'd said at Madge's earlier that afternoon. My darling little cherub was not as easily distracted as I thought.

CHAPTER 16

The sun was having a hard time penetrating the clouds Friday morning as I drove toward town to drop Peggy Lou off at Madge's house. I'd decided to spend the morning at the office to catch up on paperwork. The year was turning out to be one in which businesses flourished in Delta County. As a result, my agency had received several calls that week from people wanting to engage us for one reason or another. I'd been selective, agreeing only to assignments Bert could easily handle and nothing that would interfere with my involvement in the Grimes' property issue.

I had in mind taking the afternoon off when I finished at the office. Laundry had been piling up all week, and I wanted to get it out of the way in order to have some leisure time to spend with Buzz the next day. I figured Madge could use a break too. It had been a disturbing week for all of us.

As soon as we arrived, I told her my plan. She said she would be glad to have the time to do some shopping. Then I asked if she'd mind taking care of Peggy Lou while Buzz and I attended the art show at

Claudine's gallery the next evening. She graciously consented.

"While we're talking about schedules," Madge said, "don't forget I have an appointment with my optometrist Monday afternoon. I need to have my cataracts checked. Night driving is almost impossible now."

"I won't forget."

A popular morning children's program was playing on the TV. Peggy Lou settled herself down in front of it with Wilbur and Jeff at her side and was soon engrossed in watching colorful puppets singing lively songs. I had a sudden recall of watching Bozo as a child. For some reason I never understood, my dad detested the program. He always made me change the channel. As soon as he got busy in another room, I'd change it back.

Madge walked outside with me as I prepared to leave. "Any news about that escaped convict?" she asked, concern etched on her face.

"No, but I expect they'll apprehend him soon." I opened the door to the Explorer and gave her a smile. "A thug like him can't go undetected for very long. He's bound to cause a problem and they'll nab him." I got in, snapped my seatbelt and waved as I backed out of her driveway.

I circled the block around the office twice, looking for signs of anything unusual before pulling into the parking lot. In spite of what I'd said to Madge, the fact that Buck Harper was still on the loose made me uneasy.

I went in, disabled the alarm system, and made a pot of coffee. Bert had finished the background checks for the local bank and another for a business in Delta. Since her work was caught up, she'd taken the day off to prep for a weekend of hiking. The only thing left for me was to review the information she'd located and complete the final reports. Her work was so thorough it didn't take long to finish, leaving me extra time to tidy the office, and make a quick trip to the store to replenish supplies.

When I arrived to pick up my daughter at noon, Madge had prepared grilled cheese sandwiches, carrot sticks and chocolate cookies for lunch. It was a nice surprise.

Peggy Lou was gaining skill at climbing, and as soon as I put our plates on the table, she decided to scale the legs of her high chair to seat herself. Watching her made me tense, ready to rescue her if needed, but she squirmed her way into the seat and sat proudly smiling at me. I placed her plate before her and cut her sandwich into quarters before seating myself.

Madge brought glasses of iced tea for us and took a seat next to me. I'd no sooner taken the first bite of my own sandwich when I felt Jeff nudge my hand under the table. Begging was a practice we discouraged, but it's

111

hard to be tough when looking at those sad brown eyes. Knowing he loved cheese, I broke off a corner of my sandwich and gave it to him. He swallowed it and hunkered down at my feet to wait for another handout.

Madge glanced at him. "Wilbur and I enjoy having your dog's company, but it breaks my heart to hear him whimper when you leave him behind. I think you should take him home with you, at least for the weekend."

"We miss him too." I reached down to scratch the base of one of his ears.

As soon as Peggy Lou finished her chocolate cookie, I gathered her extra belongings and we went out to leave. Jeff sat in the doorway next to Madge. I opened the back of the SUV. "Come on, boy," I said, and slapped my thigh. He jumped to his feet, charged forward, and leaped into the Explorer, his big pink tongue registering his excitement.

Once home and out of the car, he didn't lose a minute, circling the yard marking the perimeter, then climbed the steps to the deck at the back of the house. He positioned himself at his usual lookout post, like a king surveying his domain—one happy dog.

Peggy took her usual afternoon nap while I tackled the laundry. And so Friday morphed into Saturday.

One of the benefits of working for myself was that I had control of my hours and could spend weekends with my family. Buzz was off duty, but unlike me, he didn't linger in bed that morning. He got up at the usual time and went out to take care of his horses. I roused a little later, heard him start his truck and drive away. I figured he'd gone after something he needed for the horses. He'd already returned by the time Peggy Lou and I were up and dressed. We were enjoying breakfast when he came in.

"Kevin should be here soon," he said, as he gave us each a kiss. He poured himself a cup of coffee, and headed out the door to go down to the corral. Kevin was a boy in the neighborhood who arrived promptly at eight o'clock to muck out the stable, the work in trade for riding lessons Buzz was giving him. While they were busy, Peggy Lou and I made a trip to the local grocery store to get chocolate chips to make cookies for lunch. She helped with the baking by pouring the luscious brown chips into the batter. After that she lost interest, and went to watch cartoons on TV.

With chores taken care of, at noon the three of us gathered on the deck for lunch. The big pine on the south side of the house protected us from the sun, and a breeze from the north made it a pleasant place to relax. When Peggy had eaten her fill, she found a ball and enticed Jeff into a game of fetch while we settled into our favorite lounge chairs.

Buzz unlaced his shoes and pulled them off. He leaned back and drained the last swallow of his favorite beer. "I'm thinking I'll look for a different position at work."

"This job hasn't turned out like you thought, I guess."

He grimaced and took a deep breath. "The benefits are better and my base salary is more, but by the time everything is taken out, my take-home is the same. Plus I'm spending more on travel."

I didn't know what to say, so I kept quiet. I made a point of not advising him on his career, especially since I didn't expect his advice on mine.

"I think I'd like the canine unit," he said. "I like animals better than people."

His last comment made me smile. He was the sort who could easily spend all day with his horses.

"You want another beer?" I asked.

He shook his head.

I poured myself a second glass of iced tea from the pitcher on the table. "Anything new on Hester McKay's murder?"

"I talked to Ed Bornaman, he's the lead detective, and explained my interest in the case. He said he'd let me know when the results of the preliminary post were in. He also said they plan to talk to her old boyfriend, Eddie Lee.

"He'd be first on my list of suspects, if he's been paroled." I gathered the dishes and took them to the kitchen. When I returned and sat down, he asked, "Any luck finding that deed for the Grimes Corporation?"

"Not yet, but I've accumulated enough information, I shouldn't have any trouble locating it on Monday."

We lapsed into silence, enjoying the quietude. After several minutes, Buzz reached over and took my hand. "It's probably time for our daughter to take her nap, don't you think?" He lifted his eyebrows and grinned.

"I do, indeed. Peggy Lou! Naptime."

Buzz leaned forward and picked up his shoes. "I'm going to go take a shower. You could join me, if you like."

CHAPTER 17

The sky had clouded over by the time Buzz and I left for the exhibition at Claudine's Gallery. Before we reached Delta, I wondered if we'd get another little thunder storm, and wished I'd brought a coat. I'd settled on a black skirt and white satin blouse to wear to the event. I hoped I wasn't overdressed. Buzz was wearing dark blue Dockers, a striped shirt with an open neck, and his western boots. I hoped he wasn't underdressed.

The parking lot was nearly full when we arrived leaving us a good distance to walk if it did decide to rain. I could see the posters still decorated the glass front of the building, plus a string of colored lights had been added to give a party atmosphere.

A teenage girl opened the door for us and handed me a program with a picture and lengthy background information about the featured artist, Laura Valenzuela, plus a list of local artists also displaying their work.

As if by magic, the gallery had been transformed overnight with room dividers brought in to create individual displays. The bare areas I'd seen on the walls the day before had been filled with a colorful array of oil paintings. A wicker settee and a couple of side tables stood off to one side, a comfortable place where people could sit and chat.

Someone had done a huge amount of work to pull it together. Two amber lights installed over the buffet in the back of the room made the display of food very appealing. A couple of the nicer restaurants in town were offering various hors d'oeuvres and cookies, along with an assortment of wines. Next to the buffet, a harpist, Sue Parker, the program said, was playing. The room was crowded, but not so much that visitors couldn't get a good view of each group of paintings.

Claudine rushed up to greet us. She'd chosen a stunning purple lace dress with three-quarter length sleeves and matching heels. Her honey-blonde hair, swept back and fastened with a clip, made her earrings, likely amethyst, standout.

"This is quite a transformation," I said with a wave of my hand to indicate the room.

"Thank you. I was so lucky. Laura followed the truck from Bakersfield and stayed to help. We never could have finished, if it hadn't been for her."

I introduced Buzz and she reached out to grasp his hand. "I'm so glad you could make it," she said, then motioned to the buffet. "There's food and wine. Help yourself."

A dark-haired man in an expensive-looking, tailored suit and designer tie walked over and stood next to Claudine. With his proximity, she turned. "Please meet my husband, Rick."

He grinned at us and shook Buzz's hand with enthusiasm. "Glad you could come. This is great. Several of my clients are here." His gaze scanned the room. "Supervisor Westerman said he would try to stop by. Oh, I see Larry. Excuse me." He gave Buzz's shoulder a pat and hurried off to shake hands with someone else.

I glanced around to see if Cliff Jessup had arrived. I didn't see him.

"I want you to meet Laura," Claudine said as she took my arm and pulled me toward her friend, who'd chosen black slacks and a long-sleeved, red silk blouse for the occasion. A two-strand necklace of creamy pearls and matching earrings added to the eye-catching ensemble.

After being introduced to the artist, Buzz said, "I'm going to check out the buffet. I see Joe Cline. Hey, Joe. I didn't know you were an art aficionado."

Though I enjoyed viewing all kinds of artwork, I had little knowledge of the skill that went into it. It made it hard to make small talk with the artist. I asked how long she'd known Claudine. They both laughed and Laura responded, "We met two years ago when Claudine tripped over my foot during a workshop put on by Henry Gustafson. She almost sat in my lap."

A bearded man came up to Laura and grabbed her hand, grinned and wrapped an arm around her shoulder. He pulled her away to discuss a painting. Claudine excused herself, so I drifted around the corner to view some landscapes of local sites. I took my time, moving from one to another, until I'd circled the entire room and was studying a large abstract piece resting on an easel.

Off to my right, Fillmore and Claudine stood with their heads inclined, voices low. The buzz of other conversations drowned out most of what they were saying, but when a momentary lull occurred, I heard Claudine ask, "Who the hell invited her, I want to know."

Fillmore shrugged. "Not me."

"Did you see? She's flashing Mother's ring. How could he do that? It's an insult."

"Dad wasn't the sentimental type. Mom picked out the ring. Dad just paid for it."

"I don't care. It makes my blood boil."

She was looking past me at someone near the entrance.

"Don't let her spoil things," Fillmore said. "Ignore her."

I edged around to see if I could spot the person they were talking about. A newcomer had arrived, a slender woman in a red and black strapless dress. Her long black hair brushed the red scarf draped over her shoulders. As she pointed to one of the paintings, light glinted off a ring on her left hand. I wondered who she was, and if she were part of the Grimes family.

"I need a drink," Fillmore said, and pulled away from Claudine's hand on his coat sleeve. He wound his way through the crowd until he reached a wine bottle perched in a bucket of ice at the end of the buffet table. He picked up a plastic glass from a stack and poured himself a generous drink.

A man with google-eyed glasses hurried up to him. I recognized him as the guy who'd nearly knocked me off my feet during my first visit to the headquarters. Will Grimes. He was a good deal shorter than Fillmore and had to look up at him.

"You just couldn't wait, could you. I see you got all your stuff moved. Your father's barely cold in his grave and you're taking over his office, like you're entitled."

"Oh, Willie. Relax. Have a glass of wine."

"You think you've pulled the rug out from under me, do you?" He grabbed the glass out of Fillmore's hand.

The older man drank the contents, plunked the glass on the table top, his face flooded red. He glared at his nephew. "We'll see what the board has to say about this." He turned on his heel and marched away.

I turned my head, not wanting any of them to realize I'd overheard, and found myself looking at a medium-sized painting of a house overshadowed by trees. It carried Claudine's signature in the lower right-hand corner. It was the Craftsman house I'd seen the day before, not far from the Grimes' offices.

I heard a "humph" from someone who'd come up behind me, and turned to see a thin, gray-haired lady who appeared to be about Madge's age. She tilted her head back and studied the painting through bifocals. Her grave expression made me wonder if she was an art critic.

"It looks like a nice place to live," I said, "peaceful and secluded."

"You wouldn't like it if it was *your* home on display."

"Oh. Is that your house? It's lovely."

"Humph." She spun around and moved off, ending up next to Will Grimes, who'd motioned to her. He took her by her elbow and led her away from the main gathering. They disappeared behind one of the room dividers.

A gallery staff member sidled up to me. I could tell she was part of the staff because she wore a pin on her shirt that said so. "Are you interested in the old Grimes residence?"

"Was that older woman Vivian Grimes?" I asked, indicating her departure.

She nodded. "The house has a very interesting history."

"Is that so."

"Oh, yes. It's reputed to be haunted."

"Really? By whom?"

She stepped closer, and with an air of a confidant, said, "Claudine's mother committed suicide there."

I gave her a look that was meant to convey my disbelief.

She shrugged. "Could be it's just a rumor. People like stories about old houses."

"Makes a good sales pitch, I suppose."

I turned away to look for Buzz. He and his friend were conversing next to a painting of two horses with their heads poised over a fence railing. I wiggled my fingers at him, a hint that I was ready to leave, but he gave me an absent-minded wave in return, so I sauntered over to the buffet. I helped myself to a glass of ginger ale and a cinnamon cookie. Claudine stood at the end of the table with a wine glass in her hand. By the set of her jaw, I could see she was still upset.

I glanced across the room. In the opposite corner, a chubby older lady in a blue sweater sat behind a glass showcase containing handmade jewelry. I'd cruised the entire selection of art work, so I drifted over to look at the jewelry, turquoise set in silver, beautiful, but priced far above my budget. I was tempted by a pair of earrings and was about to ask to see them, when I heard Claudine's voice coming from near the buffet.

"You've no right to my mother's ring."

I stepped around a room divider to see what was happening. The lady I thought was Vivian Grimes stood behind Claudine. They were both glaring at the woman in the red-and-black strapless. Claudine picked up a glass of wine and tossed the contents into the woman's face, then started clawing at her hand. "You whore! Take it off! Take it off!"

The disturbance sent Rick Morales rushing across the room in that direction. All heads turned. Eyebrows raised.

My reaction? I guess the party's over.

CHAPTER 18

The shock on the young woman's face was classic: eyes blinking, mouth open, gaping at the front of her dress. As though unable to process what happened, she stood frozen to the spot for about three seconds. Then, as if jarred alert, she grabbed a wine bottle and was about to clobber Claudine. But Morales intervened, seized Claudine by the arm and pulled her through a door at the back of the room.

Whispers of disbelief could be heard. The young woman set the bottle back on the buffet table. Vivian, stone-faced, stepped over to her and said something. The younger woman's eyes widened and she lifted her chin, giving Vivian a look that should have turned her to salt.

The younger woman didn't make a response, but hiked her purse strap onto her shoulder, and glanced right and left as though checking to see if people were looking at her. Whatever Vivian said had the desired effect. With her chin still in a defiant pose, she made a most nonchalant exit of the building.

Some folks watched her leave while others turned away, embarrassed for her. Once the door closed behind her, the comments gained volume.

I looked around for Fillmore and found him relaxed on the settee. I walked over and eased down next to him. "What was that all about?"

He gave a chuckle. "I'm not sure who hates Bobbie Castro more, Claudine or Aunt Vivian. Bobbie is, or was, my father's mistress, slash fiancé. They were supposed to get married as soon as he got back from his trip. Last month they threw an engagement party to let family and friends know about the upcoming nuptials. It was probably her idea." He drained the glass he'd been holding. "I need a refill." He pushed to his feet, then turned back to me with a grin. "Don't go away. There's more to the story." He made a beeline for the buffet table.

A pall had taken over the room. I waited and watched as a few of the guests shook hands with the featured artist and edged toward the door.

Fillmore soon returned and sat down again. He'd loosened his tie.

"What's the big objection to your father remarrying?" I asked. "She's quite a bit younger, but that's not so unusual."

"Easy answer." He took a swallow from the glass he held. "Money. I wasn't concerned, but Aunt Vivian and Uncle Willie figured she might have an influence on his decision-making. Plus she'd be in line to inherit a chunk of the business in the event of his death. Wouldn't be the first time a young chick came along and ended up with the whole shebang. Claudine just couldn't stand the idea of another woman living in Mom's house."

He leaned toward me, a devious smile on his lips. "I'll tell you a secret, though, something I haven't mentioned to anyone. The day before Dad took off on that trip to Arizona, he called me into his office for some last minute instructions about spraying needed on a block of Valencias. Before I left, he told me the engagement was off. He'd kicked Bobbie out of the house the night before. He didn't elaborate about the cause, but I suspect Mom's diamond ring had something to do with it."

He slouched against the back of the settee. "I figured she'd divorce him after a few years and clean house. Told him so and recommended a pre-nup. He got mad and said it was none of my business." He shrugged. "Guess I better get someone over to change the locks at the house. This could get sticky."

"Where did they live?"

"About a quarter mile from our offices on the west side of the walnut grove."

"Who lives in that lovely Craftsman just north of your offices?" I already knew, but wanted to find out if the suicide was pure rumor.

"Aunt Vivian. After Dad built the new house for Mom, Aunt Vivian and Uncle Leonard moved into Granddad's old home."

"I heard it's haunted."

Fillmore chuckled. "No ghosts. Skeletons maybe, but Aunt Viv would never tolerate a ghost. She'd send it packing."

I saw Buzz tap his wristwatch and tip his head toward the exit.

"It looks like my husband is ready to leave." I stood. "My aunt is taking care of our daughter. We need to pick her up before bedtime. Nice talking to you."

"Sure thing. We'll invite you to our next family feud." He lifted his wine glass in salute.

I joined Buzz who was shaking hands with his colleague, Joe Cline.

"Be sure to come out to watch the K9 trials next Saturday," Joe said. "It's something to see."

"I'll do that," Buzz said. "Sounds great." Buzz took my hand.

"Wait," I said. "I need to say goodbye to Claudine." I looked around the room for her, but she was nowhere in view. We weren't the only people leaving. Laura Valenzuela was stationed by the door, shaking hands and thanking people for coming.

When we were out on the pavement, I looped my arm through his. "That is some family," I said. "You should hear what Fillmore Grimes told me."

Buzz snorted. "The only difference between them and any other family is money. More money, more jealousy."

CHAPTER 19

"From what I've heard," I told him, "control of the corporation is what's causing the uproar." As we walked across the parking lot, I glanced at the sky. The moon was hidden behind thick clouds. Buzz produced a little flashlight attached to his keys and turned it on to guide our way. He unlocked the SUV and we climbed in. "What was the cat fight all about?"

"A ring. Claudine's mother's ring. I guess Claudine resents Bobbie Castro's place in her father's life."

"That's what you see on the surface." He started the engine and maneuvered through the parking lot to the freeway entrance. "I just imagine there's a lot more to it, if you could dig deeper."

"You're probably right. From what Fillmore has told me, his Uncle Will thinks he should have the reins of the corporation since he is the oldest male in the family and manages the accounts. But Fillmore thinks that as Tony's son, he's the heir apparent. There's some kind of meeting coming up where everyone is going to choose sides and vote. I'm so curious to know if they work out their differences, I think I'll almost be sorry when I find the old land records and my relationship with them comes to an end."

Buzz chuckled. "There'll probably be a court battle, then you can read about it in the newspaper."

We rode in silence for several minutes, then Buzz said, "I had a call from Troy Chapman. He has a nice pony he wants me to see. A couple of months ago I told him to keep an eye out for one. I think we should go have a look at it tomorrow."

Troy and Gracie Chapman were friends of ours. We used to double date in high school. Since then, they'd established a horse ranch northwest of town. Gracie was one of the few friends I made in Four Creeks during the year before graduation when Dad and I lived with my grandparents.

"You're a little big to be riding a pony, don't you think?"

He gave me a disdainful look. "It's not for me. It's for Peggy Lou."

I nearly choked. The thought of my child on a horse, even a small one, made my palms sweat. His announcement hit me like a jolt from a cattle prod. I didn't dare speak for fear of sounding as panicked as I felt.

When we pulled into Madge's driveway and stopped, Buzz turned in the seat and looked at me. "What's the matter? Just because you're scared of horses doesn't mean she can't learn to ride. It's not like she'll be ready tomorrow. Both she and the pony will learn together, and I'll be watching every minute."

I didn't respond. I was too busy sorting through my churning emotions.

We got out of the SUV and walked toward the front door. "You know, if you gave yourself a chance, you could get over your fear," he said as he gave the door a gentle knock with his knuckles.

The lock clicked and Madge opened it. Inside, the sound of the T.V. had been turned low, and Peggy was asleep on Madge's couch.

Madge smiled at us. "She hasn't been asleep long. How was the art exhibit?"

"Interesting," I said. "Very interesting."

Buzz scooped Peggy up in his arms, and I opened the door again. "Thank you so much," I said. "I'll tell you all about it later. We better get her to bed."

Madge blinked a couple of times, her sharp eyes studying me. She knew me too well, sensing something wasn't right. Her smile shifted, the crease between her eyes deepening.

I blew her a kiss as we went out the door and it closed behind us.

It rained during the night, starting about midnight. I heard it because I was awake imagining my baby daughter falling off the pony Buzz intended to buy. I couldn't shake the feeling of dread, in spite of his assurances.

Memories came unbidden. The summer I turned fourteen, Kara Sanders, my best friend, and I rode horses her uncle owned along an abandoned airfield in Ortega County where we lived. Neither of us were expert riders, but we were having a good time. She challenged me to a race and took off down the cracked tarmac. Moments later, her horse got tangled in barbed wire hidden in the tall weeds that had grown up where the deteriorated asphalt ran out. The horse stumbled and Kara went flying. She landed on her head, her neck broken. She died on the spot.

For many months afterward, I relived the scene in my dreams. As I listened to the rain on the roof, it returned to me in vivid detail. It was something I hadn't shared with Buzz. If I told him, would it make a difference?

Sunday afternoon found the three of us tucked into Buzz's pickup headed for Chapman's horse ranch. On the way I got up the courage to tell him about what had happened to Kara. I couched it in terms I figured Peggy wouldn't understand, but Buzz would.

When I finished, he reached over and squeezed my arm. "In all my years of teaching kids to ride, several have fallen off their horses, but none have been seriously injured." He shook his head in dismay. "You should have told me before. I sympathize with your feelings, but really, the two of you were inexperienced and should have had more supervision. That's not the way things are going to be for our child." He squeezed my arm again and gave Peggy Lou a fatherly smile.

We pulled into Chapman's driveway. Back by the stables, my friend Gracie stood holding the lead rope of a brown and white pony, a Shetland, I guessed. It reminded me of ponies I'd seen at carnivals where children rode them around in circles while their parents took snapshots as they smiled and waved.

Buzz parked and lifted Peggy out of her car seat. He stepped out to the ground and put Peggy Lou down on her feet, then walked over to where Gracie held the pony. I climbed out and followed. Troy came out of the stable to join us, and Buzz and he shook hands.

"She's about eight years old," Troy said with a motion toward the pony. "I brought her in yesterday morning."

Buzz approached the animal, offering the back of his hand for the pony to smell. Peggy looked around at me where I had stopped next to the corral fence. I tried to keep my expression neutral.

As Buzz reached to examine the creature, she shifted her hindquarters with a little sideways motion of its hooves. Troy took the lead rope from his wife. "She's a little skittish yet. Still getting used to her new surroundings."

None of what the pony did fazed Buzz. He put his hand under her jaw and lifted her lip, exposing her teeth. Then he ran his hand over her withers, along her back and down her hind legs. He lifted one hoof, gave it a glance, nodded and released it. "She looks in good shape," he said. "Has she worked with children?"

"Oh, hell yes," Troy said. "She was owned by a family with four kids. The kids have outgrown her, so the parents decided to sell."

"Does it have a name?"

"Buttercup."

Buzz nodded, walked back to where Peggy Lou was standing in front of me. He picked her up. "Want to meet Buttercup?"

He carried her toward the pony. When they got within three feet of the animal, Peggy buried her face in his shoulder. "No."

Buzz stepped closer and stroked the pony's mane and scratched behind one of its ears. "See, nice horsey."

Peggy turned her head and risked a quick peek. The animal picked that moment to give its head a vigorous shake and blew air through its nose and lips, making a snorting sound.

"No!" Peggy wrapped her arms around Buzz's neck in a death grip, squirming as she peered over his shoulder and reached an arm out for me, her face puckered in a grimace. "Mommy!"

That put me in motion. With no more than ten steps, I took her from her father's arms. "Maybe she's a little too young for this," I said.

We rode back home in silence.

What followed later that night in the privacy of our bedroom was our first serious disagreement. I got a lecture about how I shouldn't coddle my child, that it would make her weak. I asserted that she was only three, that protecting her from a traumatizing experience was hardly coddling. The heat in the room was palpable. We went to bed in a stalemate.

What I didn't find out until later was that Buzz had already paid for the animal.

CHAPTER 20

Sleep didn't come easy. I heard it raining during the two hours I spent going over and over our argument, thinking about what I'd said, and how I might have said it better. Protecting Peggy Lou was my only goal. Why couldn't Buzz see that? He'd sounded more like a cop than my husband.

I've heard that money is what most married couples fight about. In our case, Peggy Lou was more important than money. I felt him turn over several times before I finally drifted into a sleep populated by psychedelic ponies.

Later, as the sky began to lighten, I roused and was aware of him leaving the room. I knew he'd be making his own breakfast; it was his custom. Then he'd see to the care of his horses.

When I heard the back door close, I got up. Feeling sort of hung over and owlish, I slipped on a robe and went to the kitchen where I poured myself a cup of coffee from the carafe Buzz always left. I was working on my second cup when he walked in thirty minutes later. Hunched over like a gargoyle, I avoided eye contact.

He refilled the mug he'd left on the counter. "I got to thinking," he said. "I was trying to remember when Becky first started learning to ride. It took me a while, but I think it was before she started kindergarten."

I glanced up as he lifted the cup to his lips and took a sip. Becky was Buzz's daughter from his first marriage. She was attending college in Sacramento, planning to be a teacher. On occasion, he'd mentioned that before the family split up, he thought she had the makings of a fine horsewoman.

I took a deep breath. "Every child is different," I muttered, slouching again. At least that's what I'd read in those childcare books I'd poured over before Peggy Lou was born. "Some frighten more easily than others." Was he trying to relive those earlier years? Peggy Lou couldn't be a substitute for his first child. She was a real person in her own right.

He walked over to the sink, poured the remainder of his coffee down the drain and put the mug in the dishwasher. He stood with his back to me. "I guess we could wait a year. I called Troy. As soon as he finds another buyer for the pony, he'll refund the money."

I heaved a sigh of relief, that is, until it dawned on me that he'd purchased the pony even before showing it to me, and that everything that had gone on out at Chapman's, Troy's explanation, Buzz's exam of the pony, had been for my benefit. He'd already seen the animal. That's where Buzz had gone the previous morning when he'd driven away in his pickup.

I felt heat crawl up the back of my neck. I was about to open my mouth with some caustic words, when he turned around. He came over to where I was sitting at the dinette.

"I want to share my love of riding with our little girl. The lessons can wait. But in the meantime, I want you to work on getting over your fear. It's not fair to hand your baggage over to our daughter." He ran his index finger across my cheek and tweaked my earlobe, then turned to go down the hall to the bedrooms.

Peggy Lou appeared in the hallway, rubbing one eye with her fist. The lower half of her nightgown was wet. She hadn't wet herself at night in almost a year.

I straightened my back, looked up at Buzz and deliberately raised my eyebrows. "A nightmare," I whispered. He returned a curt nod and proceeded down the hall to change for work.

A half hour later, I had Peggy Lou cleaned up, sitting in her high chair and busily eating her morning cereal. Buzz appeared, buckling his cop gear around his waist. He leaned over and gave Peggy a kiss on her cheek. She giggled. He smiled as he moved to the back door, ready to leave.

"Wait!" I jumped out of my chair, flung my arms around his neck and kissed him. I couldn't let him walk out the door with bad feelings between us. It might be the day he'd never come home again.

CHAPTER 21

I was still feeling a bit edgy on the drive into town. The fact that Buzz had bought the pony without consulting me was something I'd have to deal with sometime soon. But for the time being, I decided to set the matter aside and focus on business.

As soon as I arrived at the office, I turned on the computer, unlocked my desk, and stuffed my purse into the bottom drawer. Carrying the pistol everywhere with me was getting tiresome. It occurred to me to leave it secured in the glove box of the SUV, but if the need arose, it wouldn't do me any good out in the parking lot. The fact that Buck Harper hadn't been seen in almost a week made me wonder if I needed to carry it at all.

I extracted the Grimes folder from the file cabinet and stared at it. After the events of the last few days, having another go at the courthouse records didn't sound appealing. I plopped the file on my desk and tried to think of a delaying tactic. Perhaps a jelly doughnut and some hazelnut-flavored coffee would improve my outlook. I pulled a few dollars out of my wallet and stuffed them in my pants pocket.

It's thought to be unwise to sooth your troubles with high-calorie treats, but I'd missed my usual breakfast toast. At least that was my excuse.

Over at our kitchenette, I pulled the lid off the coffee canister and discovered it contained barely enough for one pot. Making a mental note to pick up some on my way home, I poured the last of it into Mr. Coffee. I'd just pressed the start button when I heard the door open and Bert came in. She walked, or I should say limped, like she had burrs stuck between her toes.

"Would I be right if I guessed you've been on another hiking trip?"

She plopped her handbag on her desk and groaned. "Yes. Our group went to Kings Canyon on Saturday, hiked up to Mist Falls, and then on to camp at Paradise Campground for the night. It rained buckets. I woke about 2 a.m. thinking I'd go use the privy, turned over and discovered my air mattress was sitting in water. I didn't dare get up. I had no idea what the conditions were like outside my tent. I had to wait till daylight. By then the rain had stopped, but the front lip of my tent still had water caught in it and everything was wet."

"Sounds like one of the many reasons why I have no desire to go camping."

"I've got my gear hanging on a rope between two trees in my backyard to dry out."

"Maybe you should take up some other hobby, like basket weaving or yoga."

Bert shook her head. "No, no. I've been wanting to do this for ten years. It was miserable, but I got some great pictures of the falls. I'm going to have one of them blown up and framed to hang over the couch in my living room."

I filled a mug with coffee and held it out to her.

She took it, said thanks and settled at her desk.

"I was about to go next door to buy a jelly doughnut," I said. "I need a sugar-boost before I set out for the courthouse to find the Grimes land records. Can I tempt you?"

"You bet. I'm sure I must have burned enough calories Saturday to warrant an indulgence." She took a sip of coffee. "By the way, how was the art show?"

"More entertaining than I expected," I said as I went to the door. "I'll tell you when I get back."

The doughnut shop is only a few dozen steps from my office, a terrible temptation best controlled by avoiding it and its aroma of fresh-baked pastries altogether. When I entered the building, I zeroed in on the display case where a dozen or so people were milling around, pointing and making selections. But then I saw Irma Foster. I thought, oh no, not her, not on a Monday morning. I made a quick U-turn and almost reached the exit when she spotted me.

She waved the white bakery sack in her hand. "Deena," she called as she hurried toward me. "I haven't seen you in months. When are you going to bring my little great-niece over for a visit. I'm dying to see who she looks like now."

Irma is my aunt—sort of. The trouble with a family tree is you don't get to pick the branches. She and my birth mother, Lottie Weston, were half-sisters. It's a complicated tale, based on her mother's death-bed confession. According to Irma, Lottie's father and Irma's mother were a little careless during a brief affair. I wouldn't have believed it, except that Lottie left Irma a bequest in her will. But that's not why I avoided her.

When it came to Irma, one quickly felt like being sucked into a vortex of bizarre logic. She's an inveterate gossip, spies on her neighbors, and is eager to share her observations with me in particular. Worst of all, she thinks she's being helpful with her revelations . And then there's her taste in apparel. That morning she'd chosen blue jeans, the latest style with ragged holes in the knees. The orange knit shirt she was wearing bordered on exposing her midriff. And she'd gotten a tattoo. Something resembling her dog's face peeked out from under her sleeve. The ensemble was one rarely seen on a woman approaching seventy years.

I edged toward the order counter, hoping to make a quick purchase and escape Irma's latest revelation, but was blocked by an obese man in grease-splotched coveralls.

"Oh, Deena. I have the most exciting news." She was grinning like she'd just won the lottery. "I had my DNA done. You'll never guess. We're German and English with a little bit of American Indian."

"What do you mean, 'we're'?" Sharing DNA with her was something I found less than appealing.

Her eyes went wide, her face registering surprise at my response. "Why, you and me, we share the same genes."

The man in mechanic's coveralls took his bag of baked goods and stepped aside. I placed my order with the white-aproned clerk, then turned back to Irma.

"I guess we do share some genetic background, but not from your mother's line." I knew because I'd become well versed on the issue of DNA some time back, when I'd served as a juror for a paternity trial.

She blinked a couple of times, a quizzical look forming on her face. "What do you mean?"

"Your DNA tracks your mother's genes, then her mother's, your great grandmother's and so on. You see, it doesn't have any connection to me."

By her narrow-eyed expression, I could see she was processing what I'd said. It took about five seconds. "You mean they didn't test for my father's genes?" She gave a huff. "Well, I never. I want my money back." Her jaw jutted forward, and without saying goodbye, she strode to the exit and gave the door a push I feared would loosen the hinges. I had a sudden precognition that someone was going to have a hard time explaining the particulars of DNA testing to my science-challenged aunt.

Back at the office Bert and I feasted on the sticky doughnuts and a second cup of coffee while I entertained her with a blow-by-blow description of the Grimes family squabble at the art show. Her response was similar to Buzz's.

"Power and wealth are a combination that rarely fails to bring out the worst in people," she said. She folded her napkin and stood to take her cup to the sink.

"It's true, but I have to say that in spite of it, I kind of like them. Well, maybe not their Aunt Vivian. I never saw the woman smile, even before the row."

I drained the last swallow of coffee and gathered the crumbs of frosting from the doughnut. "I must go," I said with resignation. "Those county records aren't going to come to me."

CHAPTER 22

When I walked into the Records Office Monday morning, I found a different clerk behind the glass barrier, a gray-haired woman with a round face. She smiled at me as I explained my quest, then pointed behind me. "All of our historical records have been microfilmed."

I looked over my shoulder and saw a bank of vertical file cabinets I hadn't noticed when I walked in.

"You'll need to know the name of the owner, because they're filed by name."

I looked back at her. "Are they alphabetical?"

"Some of them, but not all. You'll just have to search."

I walked over to take a look. The cabinets were the type specifically designed for microfilm storage, six feet tall with three layers of pull-out files, and each with a label on the outside. I located the earliest date available, pulled open the drawer and found a row of film boxes, each a half-inch wide. After selecting one, I turned to one of the microfilm readers lined up on a long narrow table opposite the files. I'm not unfamiliar with microfilm readers, but it seems like each of them is a little different. I had to resort to reading the directions before I had the film threaded correctly.

With a little adjustment, I was soon reading documents from the 1860s, most written in flowery handwriting. Over the next hour and a half, I slowly wound my way through five rolls of film and was beginning to feel discouraged. I rubbed the back of my neck and took a deep breath before loading another roll.

My head was aching from the eyestrain when at last I saw the name I recognized—Fillmore B. Grimes. The date was 1862, but it wasn't a deed. I squinted as I read the details.

> Approved May 20, 1862, entitled "An act to secure homesteads to actual settlers on public domain," Fillmore B. Grimes has made payment in full for S 1/2 of NW 1/4 and NE 1/4 of NW 1/4 and SW 1/4 of NE 1/4 of Section 5 in Township twenty-eight (28) N of Range twenty-four (24) E containing 160 acres.
> Now, therefore, be it known, That on presentation of the Certificate to the Commission of the General Land Office, that said Fillmore B. Grimes shall be entitled to the Tract of Land above described.
> Henry M. Atkinson Register.

I almost broke out in a cheer. When my glee subsided, I mused that if this was the only record related to the well in question, the Grimes family lore was mistaken. Their ancestor hadn't won the land in a card game, he'd homesteaded it. It didn't matter to me as the document in front of me held all the information Jessup would need to verify that the current boundaries were the same as the original.

I pressed the button to make the machine print. The first copy was too small, barely readable. With more adjustment, I finally had a good copy in my hand. I printed two more for good measure, rewound the tape and returned it to its proper place. Back at the glass barrier, I nodded to the woman, paid the fee and went out into the hall.

I headed for the exit, my thoughts running ahead of me. I'd report my find to Jessup first, find out if he wanted me to contact a surveyor, then go to the office to write my report. Before I reached the exit, I pulled my cell phone out of my purse.

I was so focused on making the call, I wasn't paying attention to my surroundings until I literally bumped into a woman as I passed through the double doors.

"I'm sorry. Excuse me," I said as a flash of blue jacket crossed my field of vision.

"Hey, watch where you're going."

I looked up to utter further apology and found myself face-to-face with Robin Masters. Her mouth formed a big O in surprise upon recognition, then her expression changed into a smirk. "Imagine running into you again."

I was just as surprised and blurted, "What are you doing here?"

"I could ask you the same question." She held up her camera. "I'm covering the Fink trial."

I hadn't noticed the other day, but now that I was standing closer to her, I could see gray streaks in her dark brown hair. I'd have to give her credit though, she looked very professional in the black slacks and tailored blue suit jacket. A label attached to her lapel read, "Press."

Her mouth twisted into a sardonic grin. "By the way, it's a good thing I didn't let Sam erase the tape he shot out at the Grimes headquarters." She lowered her voice and leaned a little closer.

My reaction was to pull away and make some cutting remark, but I restrained myself. I could listen first.

"My sources tell me," she said with a sly smile, "that the cables on Grimes' plane were deliberately damaged. The crash was no accident."

I was capable of sneering too. "Hardly new information. Fillmore Grimes already knew about the damaged cables. And who is your so-called *source*?"

"You'll never know, but let's just say it's someone *very, very* close to the NTSB." Her eyes narrowed. "Have you gotten on the inside track enough to know who has the most to gain from Tony Grimes' death?"

I wanted to say, none of your damn business, but instead, I said, "I don't think that's clear yet."

Her sculpted eyebrows lifted as well as one corner of her mouth. "Follow the money—that's what I plan to do."

"I need to make a couple of phone calls." I made a move to get around her.

"I bet you do." She quickly pulled a business card out of her jacket pocket and pushed it at me. "Here. Find out which insurance company was carrying the policy on Tony Grimes' life and let me know. There might be something in it for you."

I almost choked. "Yeah. Right. Excuse me." I pushed past her. What kind of hack did she think I was?

I was still fuming as I headed back to where I'd parked the Explorer. She was right about one thing, though. If the crash turned out to be a murder, money was bound to be mixed in there somewhere, and when I thought about the insurance policy Russ Treadwell had told me about, it sure seemed like murder was a definite possibility. I thought about the members of the Grimes family I'd met. Who *did* have the most to gain?

I sat in the SUV while I called Cliff Jessup's office to let him know I'd found the Grimes homestead papers and ask about hiring a surveyor.

"He's in court all day," his secretary told me, but I could leave a message. I declined. With all the properties the Grimes Corporation had bought and sold over the years, they probably had a surveyor they'd used before.

I called the headquarters. "Mr. Fillmore Grimes isn't in," Holly said, "but Mr. Willard Grimes is. I'll connect you."

A moment later he picked up. "Will Grimes speaking."

"Mr. Grimes, this is Deena Powers."

"You one of those investigators?" he asked, his tone demanding, impatient.

"Well, yes. I just need to know …"

"You ought to be talking to the mechanic who serviced my brother's plane. He's the one who should be investigated. If he wasn't doing a proper job of maintenance, he's liable. I don't know how he keeps his license. He's past retirement age. Tony kept using him 'cause he was an old crony of Dad's, a drinking buddy. Taught Tony and Viv flying too. Our old man thought I should learn to fly, but I wasn't interested."

"Mr. Grimes, I just need to know the name of …"

"You mean you don't know? Some investigator you are. Mike Horn's his name. He's located up in

Gateway. He overcharged too. I know because I pay the bills around here. Dang plane was an unneeded expense. Tony thought he had to fly around to keep tabs on the fields. I told him, he'd see more on the ground. Go talk to Mike Horn. Look at those maintenance records."

I wasn't getting through to him, so thanked him and hung up. It wasn't the information I was after. I decided to stop by Claudine's gallery to tell her the good news.

Once again, I'd locked my pistol in the glove box. I took it out and put it in my purse, though I didn't feel the same concern about seeing Buck Harper. I figured he'd opted for Mexico. When the investigation of Hester's murder was complete, I'd bet Eddie Lee would turn out to be the one responsible. I turned the key and headed for the freeway.

I parked near the entrance to the gallery, stuffed my pistol into the glove box and locked it. It was getting to be a drag, in and out, in and out. I got out of the car, hustled to the gallery door and pulled it open. As soon as I stepped in, I heard Fillmore's voice. "He's gone and done it again, Claudine," he was saying.

I was surprised to see both Fillmore and Claudine standing at the back of the room. Intent on their conversation, they hadn't noticed me.

"He's made an offer on another walnut orchard. We don't need more orchards. We need to diversify, grow tomatoes and specialty foods for the year-round market."

I approached them and attracted Claudine's attention. She glanced my way. "Hush. We have company." They both turned, each forcing a smile.

"I have good news," I said. "I located the original homestead claim for your ancestor's land. Now you'll only need to have a surveyor do his job, and I'm sure it will keep the dispute from ending up in an expensive court battle."

"Well, that's some consolation," Fillmore said. "With Uncle Willie buying up land like he's playing with Monopoly money, and the NTSB breathing down our necks, we could use a break."

"Have you heard anything new?" I asked.

"Not yet," he said. "I imagine the work on those control cables will take a couple of weeks."

"Fillie, you're going to have to take charge of Uncle Will," Claudine said turning her attention back to him. "He won't listen to anything I say. Talk to Aunt Viv. She's the only one he'll pay attention to. Roz Chambers is coming soon to help me inventory and crate the remaining paintings for shipment back to Bakersfield. I want to get them out of here this afternoon, so I don't have to pay for security another night."

"I'll call Aunt Viv," he said. "I managed to get the

board meeting postponed, but Sis, you've got to vote with me, or Uncle Willie's going to bankrupt us."

A cell phone chimed, and Fillmore reached for the back pocket of his jeans. He pulled out the phone and looked at its face. "Oh, crap. It's Manuel out at the packinghouse. There's been some trouble. He told me yesterday that the labor contractor is demanding extra for work after 7 P.M. He's been threatening a walkout. Excuse me." Fillmore stepped through the door in the back of the room. "Yeah, Manuel. What's happening?"

I turned my attention to Claudine. "I made copies of the homestead application off the microfilm. I have them in my bag here. Let me show you." I pulled out a copy and unfolded it. "I'll head to my office and prepare my final report. I don't think I used up the time your father thought it would take. There's likely to be a refund of unused monies."

"Yes, do that," she said. "Send your report to Cliff. I just can't deal with any more, Deena. Fillie has me in such a quandary." She put the palm of her hand on her forehead. "I have an awful headache. I just wish Uncle Will and Fillmore would quit fighting. I don't know which one of them is right. And Cliff is tied up with that stupid trial."

CHAPTER 23

There wasn't anything I could do for Claudine except sympathize, so I gave her shoulder a squeeze, told her to call if she needed me and left.

Back in the Explorer, I glanced at the clock on the dash. Madge's doctor's appointment wasn't until 1:30, which meant I had time to grab some lunch before I needed to pick up Peggy Lou. I looked around for a restaurant. Across the parking lot I spotted the Blue Ribbon Café. It was a bit farther than I cared to walk, so I turned the key in the Explorer, and a minute later coasted into the last parking space in front.

Once inside, I grabbed a menu from a caddy near the door and glanced around for a booth that was unoccupied. Most were full of people, as well as the stools along the counter in front. I concluded the food must be good. The decor was cheerful with red vinyl upholstery and framed photos of old-fashioned diners displayed on the space between the windows.

Settling in a booth near the door, I looked at the menu and debated whether to order a healthy salad or a less healthy hamburger. A dark-haired waitress approached. I looked up, ready to order and recognized

Bobbie Castro, Tony Grimes' cast-off lover. It looked like her new circumstance had forced her to get a job. She wasn't nearly as glamorous in a restaurant uniform and SAS shoes as she had been at Claudine's gallery. By her expression, I could tell she recognized me too.

"I know you," she said. "You're that investigator Tony planned to hire before his plane crashed. I saw you at the gallery the other night." She pulled her three-by-five order book out of her apron pocket. "Quite a show Claudine put on. Damned embarrassing." With a pencil from behind her ear, she poised to write. "What'll you have?"

"The number three burger."

"Fries, or green salad?"

"Salad."

"Dressing?"

"Thousand Island, on the side."

"Something to drink?"

"Lemonade."

"Good. I'll be right back with your drink."

I watched as she went to the pass-through window and clipped my order to the circular device for the cook. She then passed through a swinging door into the kitchen.

I settled back to wait and speculate about her role in the Grimes drama. Was she really the thief Fillmore had described?

She came back a couple minutes later, placed my glass of lemonade on the table and slid in onto the bench seat opposite me. She leaned her arms on the table. I noticed the absence of any rings on her slender fingers.

"I'm not the bad guy that family makes me out to be," she said. "Whatever they told you was lies. That sister of Tony's is a meddling witch. Tony and I were getting married, had it all arranged. She interfered every way she could, turned the others against me. I never did anything to them."

"I'd say the family has had a lot to deal with lately."

Her eyes misted over. She reached to grab a napkin from the napkin holder. "They aren't the only ones. I miss him, damn it, even though he could be a pain in the butt." She wiped her nose and sniffed. "I've been hearing rumors about the crash, that it might not have been just an accident." She gave me a questioning look.

"I've heard the same rumors," I said. "But they are only rumors. Crash investigations sometimes take a long time. It's unfortunate."

Behind her, I saw three customers had entered the building and were looking at a menu. She must have noticed my distraction, because she glanced over her shoulder, then turned back to me. "It's okay. My uncle owns this place. Maria will take care of them."

She was right. The other waitress, a Hispanic girl,

came from behind the counter and motioned them to an empty booth.

Bobbie leaned forward. "If the plane was sabotaged, I know who'd have a strong motive to do something like that. Tony came home in a huff a week before his trip. When I asked what had him upset, he said he was going to ask for a mid-year audit of the accounts. He wouldn't say any more, but I figure it must have had to have something to do with his brother. They were always at odds. Seems like each of them, Fillmore included, had different ideas about the future of the business. Tony wanted to expand the farm in Arizona, in fact, that's what the trip was about. He had a deal cooking over there. His brother, Will, thought they should buy up more groves around here, and Fillmore's idea was to grow fresh vegetables on the coast. Don't you see? There wasn't enough money to do it all. The bank was getting jittery about the debt they had already."

I sipped my lemonade and thought back to what Holly had said about the argument she'd heard. She thought it was about company finances.

"If the authorities conclude that the crash wasn't accidental, then perhaps you should tell them what you know. As for me, I've completed my investigation of the property records Mr. Grimes originally requested. I'll be writing my final report when I get back to my office." I didn't want to give her the idea I would be taking sides in the Grimes family squabble.

She slumped against the backrest and looked out the window, her lips forming a pouty expression.

A bell pinged, indicating another order was ready. She slid out of the booth, went to the pass-through window and returned with my hamburger. She plunked it down in front of me. "I can see you're no help," she said with disgust and walked away.

I took a deep breath and looked at my hamburger. So much for a relaxed lunch.

CHAPTER 24

Madge was dressed for her appointment when I arrived to pick up Peggy Lou. She was wearing the Vera Wang dress I'd given her for her birthday. "You're looking rather stylish for a doctor's appointment," I said.

"My appointment has been moved to 3:30. His office staffer called to make the change. I'm having lunch with Vivian Rudd. I called her the other day as you recommended. I have in mind suggesting she join the Women of Colonial Heritage. She welcomed my call, so as soon as I heard from Dr. Bell's office, I contacted her again, and we're meeting at The Wildwood Café in about ..." She glanced at her watch … ten minutes."

"Good idea." Taking care of my daughter every day had kept Madge tied down. She deserved a break. I picked up Peggy's stuffed kitten and Peggy grabbed her box of Animal Crackers. Madge is not in favor of sweets for small children, but Animal Crackers seemed to be on the acceptable list.

"See you tomorrow," I said as I hustled Peggy Lou out the door.

I noticed a car I didn't recognize, a Lexus, in our parking lot when I pulled in at the office. It wasn't a rental, so I wasn't concerned about who had been driving it. I unbuckled Peggy Lou and helped her out of the Explorer. She scampered to the office door, twisted the knob and went in. I followed.

Bert was smiling. "Looks like we're getting new neighbors," she said. "A man and woman are in there right now, checking it out."

"Any inkling who they might be?"

"Not at all, but the way she's dressed, I'd peg her as a real estate agent."

The adjoining office space had been empty for months. I hoped having a business next door would be a good thing. "As long as it's not a massage parlor, it's okay with me."

Peggy settled herself in her corner table, stuffed a couple of crackers in her mouth and opened one of her favorite coloring books.

I went into my office, pulled my notes and the copies of the homestead document out of my purse. "I found the land record for the Grimes Corporation," I said to Bert. "As soon as I send my report and an accounting to Jessup, my part of the case will be finished. I imagine the dispute will be settled out of court."

"That's good. Too bad Tony Grimes didn't live long enough to see the results," Bert replied.

161

I put my pistol-packing purse in my desk drawer and then stood in the doorway. "I hope they get a report from the NTSB soon, because rumors are buzzing around like mosquitoes."

"You mean rumors about the crash?"

"Two people have told me today that they believe the crash was intentionally rigged."

"That's murder."

"True. Further delay of a report will only make it worse, more talk, more speculation. Claudine Morales is so stressed out, she can hardly think." I reached over to turn on my computer. "The resolution of this property line issue will be one less thing for them to worry about."

I sat at my desk, focused my attention on the computer screen and spent the next half-hour preparing my report, accounting for my time, and finally, writing a refund check for unused monies. With everything tucked into an envelope, sealed and addressed, I stretched.

I glanced over at Peggy Lou. I was debating whether to take her home for her nap, or let her sleep there on the sleeping pad I'd created, when my cell phone jingled.

I tugged it out of my bag. The caller ID told me it was Buzz. I felt a rush of adrenaline. Buzz never called from work unless it was really important. I answered with, "Hi honey."

"Hi." I heard him take a deep breath. "Got some news on the McKay case."

"Good, I hope."

"I wish it were. I found out that Eddie Lee was killed in a prison yard fight a month ago. Also, the preliminary autopsy report is back. As we expected, her death was caused by a gunshot to her head, but she also had a lot of bruising on her face, arms, and legs. Like she might have been manhandled beforehand."

"You mean, like she fought back. So you think it might have been a drug deal gone bad?

"Hard to say. She didn't have the usual track marks of a junkie. The tox report will come later. The team is going back to the house tomorrow."

"It rained last night," I observed. "Any additional evidence was likely destroyed."

"I know, but I'm sure they recovered most of it the first day."

I pictured Hester, with her frizzy blonde hair, being held down with a gun to her head. It caused a sick sensation in my stomach.

A silence hung between us, then Buzz said, "Gotta go. Love you."

CHAPTER 25

I listened to the dial tone for several seconds, then disconnected and sat staring into space. I hadn't known Hester well, but her testimony had helped put Lottie's killer in prison. She deserved better.

My face must have reflected what I was feeling, because Bert said, "Bad news?"

From over in the corner, Peggy said, "Mommy?"

Jolted out of my reflections, I straighten my back and smiled at Peggy Lou. "Daddy has a hard job today, that's all. He wants you to know he loves you."

With that assurance, Peggy Lou resumed her coloring.

I pushed out of my chair, went to the office coffee bar and started rinsing my already-clean coffee mug, the mug I'd used that morning. Bert followed me. "What's going on?" she asked in a low tone.

"The McKay case. The initial post. No surprises. A homicide. The who and why, unknown." I wiped the cup with a paper towel and put it back on the shelf. "I want to go talk to her employer. Is it okay if I leave Peggy with you?"

"Sure. If she'll stay. But are you sure you should do that?"

"No." I took a deep breath. "Yes. I can't stand the way I'm feeling, helpless and agitated. I've got to move the needle."

I turned my attention to Peggy. "Hey, punkin. Mommy needs to run an errand. You can stay here with Bert for a little bit."

Peggy looked at me, her mouth full of cookie, and mumbled okay.

"I won't be long," I told her. Preparing to leave, I fetched my purse from my desk.

Hester's murder had never been far from my thoughts, and now that the Grimes assignment was completed, Buzz's call jarred it out of the back of my brain.

While parking in front of Fair Buy Market, I realized I didn't know for certain if Hester McKay was still working there before her death. I hadn't seen her during my most recent shopping trips. I went through the usual routine with the gun, got out and locked the Explorer before heading for the door.

As soon as I entered, I looked around for someone I recognized. Failing that, I approached the middle-aged clerk at the first check-out. She was in the midst of processing packages being loaded onto the conveyor by a woman dressed in shorts and a sweatshirt.

I raised my hand to get her attention. "Excuse me. I'd like to talk to the store manager."

She gave me a look designed to make me feel like a worm to ask such a thing. "Hold on," she said. When she finished with the customer's purchases, she lifted the store phone from its hook, paged him and hung it up.

The phone jingled. She reached for the receiver and said, "There's a woman here says she wants to talk to you." A second's pause, and she turned to me. "What's your name?"

I told her and pulled a business card from my pocket. She waved it off, repeating what I'd said. "He'll be right down. You can wait over in the bakery goods section." She replaced the receiver and turned away to reach for the next customer's items.

I knew where to find the bread aisle. I shopped for items there every week, though I'd never paid much attention to the door in the corner. I walked over just as it opened and Clark Weir materialized. I hadn't seen him in years. In the interim, he'd shaved his head and acquired a little paunch. His attire was standard for a store manager: tan slacks, a short-sleeved, striped shirt and blue tie. We met in front of a stack of specially priced crackers.

I held out my business card. "I don't know if you remember me. It's been a long time."

He took the card and squinted as he read it, reaching to his shirt pocket at the same time. Not finding his glasses, he said, "I thought I recognized the name when Helen said who you were."

"I wanted to inquire about Hester McKay."

"You haven't heard?"

"Yes. I know what happened to her. I was wondering if she was still working here."

"She was." He handed my card back to me. "She called in early Tuesday and quit. Didn't give a reason or anything. Just flat quit. Made me mad, giving no warning like that. I had to scramble to cover her shift."

"Had you had any problems with her beforehand?"

"No. Her attendance record was good." He ran a hand over his bald head. "Then I heard she was dead. And on top of that, one of the other girls called in sick. She's been so upset about what happened to Hester, she may need counseling. I had to pay overtime to cover those shifts."

"The girl who called in sick, were they friends?"

"I can't say. Maybe. I don't have time to keep track of my employee's personal lives."

"What's her name? Is she here?" I glanced around the area I could see. "Could I speak to her?"

"Her name's Lauren. She's in the break room. I'll check, see if she'll talk to you." He went back through the door, and in a moment, returned with a young woman who looked like a scared pup, eyes wide. I guessed her age at early twenties and gave her a reassuring smile. Her dark hair had been pulled back into a ponytail, and she wore the store's uniform with a logo patch on the sleeve. Dark circles under her eyes marred her smooth complexion and made me wonder if she was having trouble sleeping.

I stepped forward and offered my hand.

"This here's Deena Powers," Mr. Weir said. "She's a detective and wants to ask you about Hester."

Lauren took a step back and shook her head, hunching her shoulders as if someone might be about to strike her.

"I'm not with the police. I knew Hester, and I want to know what happened to her."

Tears filled Lauren's eyes. "She's dead."

"I know. I'm sorry. When did you talk to her last?"

She hesitated, maybe debating with herself about what to reveal. "The night before. We ate at Luna's Pizza to celebrate her birthday." A tear edged down her cheek. "She was *only* twenty-eight."

"Did she give any indication that she planned to quit her job?"

Lauren glanced at Mr. Weir. She shook her head.

His lips narrowed into a thin line. "Break time is over."

"I won't keep you," I said. "Is there another time we could talk?"

She moved in the direction of the check-outs. I followed along behind, hoping for an answer.

She glanced over her shoulder. "I texted her when I heard she quit." She paused at the end of the bread aisle.

I heard the door behind us close. "He's gone," I said.

She reached in her pocket, pulled out a tube of lipstick and applied a little to her lower lip. "Hester didn't return my text. It wasn't like her, so I went over to her house. We've been friends for years. Hung out on weekends. I knocked, but she didn't come to the door, so I went around to the back. The door wasn't locked. I went in." Her hand shot to cover her mouth. "I freaked when I saw her on the floor and all that blood." Her hands fluttered in front of her face. "I ran out and called 9-1-1."

Both hands covered her face for a couple seconds until I asked, "Did Hester use drugs?"

Her eyes full of tears, she sucked in a breath. "I gotta get to work or he'll be on my neck." She hurried off toward her station.

I called after her. "Did she?"

She muttered something that sounded like, "Not that kind."

What did Lauren mean, not that kind? Was she talking about pot? My head rang with questions, but didn't want to get her into trouble, so I left.

CHAPTER 26

I drove past Hester's house, then pulled over to the curb for a minute. Looking back, I saw that the yellow tape that had been draped along the bushes and from tree to tree the week before was gone. It wasn't a bad looking place, a shotgun house, as I remembered. It just needed a new coat of paint. I didn't know whether Hester owned or rented it, but if it were a rental, the owner would have a hard time finding new tenants. People tend to shy away from houses where someone's been murdered.

I pulled out and moved on, turned at the end of the block and rubbernecked as I passed the alley that ran between Elm and Chestnut. Trash cans at the back of each house meant the trash truck would be coming by soon. A trash can is sometimes a treasure trove of clues to a person's life. The police had probably searched Hester's. What did the investigators hope to find when they returned?

Somehow I couldn't quite swallow the idea of Hester being part of the drug scene. I'd watched her during Eddie Lee's trial, and though I couldn't put my finger on it, she just didn't seem the type. Logic told me there'd be nothing new to find, but I wanted to look anyway.

Circling back, I turned in and stopped where the CSI van had been parked, hoping my tire tracks would be obscured. I glanced around at the neighbor's back yards. Finding no one in view, I reached in the back seat for my hooded sweatshirt, then fished a pair of plastic gloves out of the center console and stepped out. After slipping the keys into my pants pocket, I stuffed my purse under the front seat, and donned the sweatshirt, pulling the hood over my head. If anyone saw me, they'd likely think I was a homeless person looking for aluminum cans.

As I approached Hester's trash barrels, I pulled on the gloves. The blue one would contain stuff to be recycled. Tilting it on its side, I raked some of the contents out on the lid. There wasn't much, mostly empty Del Monte cans, discarded paper cups from fast food restaurants, and empty frozen food containers. The only thing I'd learned was that Hester didn't cook much. After shoving the contents back inside the can, I stood and lifted it back up on its wheels.

The other barrel, the black one, would contain stinky stuff to go to the land fill. I lifted the lid. The contents, a mixture of coffee grounds and unmentionable items gave off an aroma that would gag a maggot, as they say. One whiff and I pitied the poor cop who'd probably had to go through it. I dropped the lid and pushed both barrels to the spot where the trash truck would empty them when it came by. My good deed for the day.

I turned around and looked at the back of the house. It was a 1940s structure with wood siding and old sash windows. A concrete walkway led from the back door to the side door of an unattached garage that bordered the alleyway. I walked over and tried the handle. It wasn't locked, so I opened it and looked inside. Light seeped in under the pull-up garage door. It was empty, except for an old wooden ladder. Either Hester didn't own a car, or the investigators took it away to be examined.

That little voice in my head told me there was nothing in the house to be discovered, but ... I still wanted to see if there was some indication that Hester had been a tweaker. It was a nutty idea. I'd have to be careful not to leave evidence of my presence. It's called breaking and entering. Definitely frowned upon by the law.

Three concrete steps led to the screened-in back porch. I approached, expecting the door to be locked. If that were the case, my invasion would end. It would be too risky to use my lock picks in broad daylight. I'd left them in my purse. However, if the door wasn't locked, it wouldn't be a B and E. I turned the knob. To my surprise, the door opened, but not without a noisy squawk.

I stepped in and crouched down, in case a neighbor might have heard and look for the origin of the sound. Everyone in town knew about Hester's murder. I counted to sixty and listened for a door somewhere in the neighborhood. Hearing nothing, I glanced around the five-by-six porch. By the looks of its condition, it had been added on after the original construction. A kitchen-sized waste basket stood in the corner. It was empty.

I doubted I'd be so lucky as to find the interior door unlocked. Still crouched, I turned the knob. It was loose, wobbly. It turned round and round in my hand, then caught and with an easy shove, it swung open. Feeling a little silly, I duck-walked into the kitchen and pushed the door closed.

When I pivoted around to stand, I came face-to-face with a dark brown stain on the vinyl flooring. Shivers spread across my shoulders. It was undoubtedly where Hester had lain as she died. I stood and skirted around it. My knees a bit shaky, I took advantage of a kitchen chair next to the table a few steps away. I averted my eyes, looked at the ceiling and took a couple of deep breaths. What was I doing there? I had to be nuts to think I'd find something a perfectly good cadre of investigators hadn't found.

Haste would be a good idea, I told myself, so I tiptoed down the short hall, like someone in the empty house was going to hear me.

I came to a ten-by-twelve bedroom on my left. From the doorway, I saw a few framed prints of flowers on the opposite wall. The double bed had been stripped bare. The bedding was piled on the floor, and the mattress a few inches off center, like someone had looked underneath. A bedside table held a lamp and a box of tissues. Dresser drawers hung open. I stepped over to take a quick look. The contents were in disarray. The thought of the investigators pawing through Hester's underwear was distasteful, even though I knew it was necessary.

Next to the dresser was the closet. I moved over to open it. It was no more than five feet in width. Her store uniform was present, along with numerous shirts hung next to a half dozen pairs of slacks. A couple of purses sat on the shelf above, both open and empty. Her shoes were neatly lined up on the floor: two pair of dress shoes, several sandals, and three pair of sneakers in varying states of wear. Unlike most people whose main focus in life was drug acquisition, Hester had kept a tidy home.

I returned to the hall, went into the bathroom and opened a cabinet door. It was almost empty. Except for a toothbrush, tube of toothpaste, shampoo, and cosmetics, any other contents had, no doubt, been carted away by the investigators.

Opposite the bathroom, a second bedroom had a single bed, the covers pulled back, mattress askew, and a chest of drawers, also opened for scrutiny. A wing-backed chair stood in one corner. An inspection of the closet revealed it to be empty.

The living room was exactly as I remembered it from the day years earlier when I'd visited Hester to make inquires about Lottie Weston. The overstuffed orange sofa and loveseat took up most of the space. The cushions had been removed and stacked in the corner.

The entire tour had taken less than ten minutes. I went back to the kitchen and looked into the sink. Other than rust stains, it was empty. The waste basket under the sink held a few empty soda cans. I studied the counter, all four feet of it, because Buzz had said there had been drug paraphernalia there. It appeared to have been wiped clean.

The fridge was an old white Kenmore. I opened it. The light came on. The contents were sparse: a jam jar, a half-full catsup bottle, three cans of diet soda, and in the door, a quart-sized milk container, the same brand I often bought. The top was open. I absently picked it up. It was empty. Why would Hester leave an empty milk carton in the refrigerator?

I closed that door and opened the freezer. Inside was an ice cube tray, a package of frozen peas and a pint container of chocolate ice cream, the lid open. I tipped it to see how much was left. It was empty, except for a plastic spoon. No woman would leave empty containers in a refrigerator, especially someone as neat as Hester. Goose bumps prickled my arms. Someone other than the police had been in the house.

A thought popped like a soap bubble. I rushed back to Hester's bedroom and lifted the mattress. The underside had been slashed and stuffing pulled out, not something investigators would do. With my pulse quickening, I went to check the sofa cushions. They'd received the same treatment. In the other bedroom, I found that the mattress had been ravaged. Without a doubt, someone had been looking for something. Drugs? Money? Was that why she was killed? Had the mattresses and cushions been sliced open before or after the police had arrived? Besides Lauren, who were Hester's other associates? To find out, I'd have to talk to Lauren again.

While I stood there with my thoughts bouncing around like a kitten after a string, I heard a faint noise coming from overhead, a scratching or paper rustling. Adrenaline surged. I looked up at the ceiling and held my breath, listening several seconds, then tip-toed into the hall where I figured the attic access would be located. The cover to the opening looked undisturbed. I stood beneath it, listening again. Not a sound. It probably was a mouse, I told myself, or maybe a bird had found some way into the attic. Whatever, I decided on a quick departure.

As quiet as a nun in a cloister, I left and got back into the SUV. Someone besides me had been in

Hester's house since the police. Who? A drug dealer? Or, worst thought of all, Buck Harper?

CHAPTER 27

That night, I dreamed I was back in high school. Robin Masters was walking by, clinging to Buzz's arm. They were both laughing. The classroom bell rang. But it didn't sound right. It was intermittent, like a warning bell—fire or something. By the fourth ring, I recognized it was the bedside phone. Tangled in the covers, I groped to reach it and croaked a "hello" into the receiver.

"Deena." Madge's quavering voice penetrated my fog. "Someone has broken into my garage. What is the world coming to?"

Fully awake, I pushed myself up on one elbow. "Call the police."

"I did. But Deena, who would care about what's in those cartons of historical records belonging to the Women of Colonial Heritage? They've been dumped out on the garage floor. It's a mess."

"I'll be there as soon as we can get dressed."

"Thank you, dear."

I replaced the receiver and focused on the bedside clock. It was early, even for Madge. Buzz wasn't home yet. He was doing an overnighter. He'd traded shifts with another officer, so his coworker could attend a wedding.

Peggy Lou appeared in the bedroom doorway hugging her grubby stuffed kitten. She must have heard the phone too. I pushed back the covers and slid my feet to the floor.

"Aunt Madge needs us to help clean up some stuff in her garage," I said. "She wants us to hurry." I hustled Peggy into the bathroom. Once she was pottied and brushed, I didn't give her a chance to fuss about what she'd wear. I stuffed her chubby legs into a pair of orange coveralls, buttoned it and carried her to the kitchen. I gave her a granola bar from the cabinet. I'm not sure, but I suspect she shared half of it with Jeff, our Dobe, while I was busy leaving a message for Bert to let her know I wouldn't be in that morning. I gathered the usual things that went with us every day, called Jeff, and hurried out to the Explorer.

With Peggy Lou in her car seat, and the dog in back, we were soon on the road to Four Creeks. Though it was only a twenty-minute drive to Madge's house, it seemed longer—one of those times I wished we lived closer to her.

If there was any damage to the old records, Madge would feel responsible, since she was the WCH registrar and historian. Her chapter had shrunk since the murder of her friend at their spring colonial tea a few years earlier. The remaining members shuffled the various offices when it came to election time. But no one wanted to be responsible for the files Madge had stored in her garage, so she held the same office for over five years.

A FCPD squad car was parked on the edge of the road in front of Madge's house when I pulled into the driveway. Madge was standing at the back garage door still wearing her favorite robe over the nightgown I'd given her for Christmas. I recognized Mike Huerta, one of Four Creeks officers, and Buzz's friend, talking to her. He had a notepad in his hand and was jotting notes as they spoke. Another officer was applying fingerprint dust to the windowsill of the garage's only window. I didn't recognize him. I decided to leave Jeff in the back of the SUV in case he took a dislike to one of the men.

While helping Peggy out of the car, I heard Madge say, "By the time I put on my robe and got to the door, he was gone. I don't know how he got away so quick unless he drove up that way." She motioned to where the road crested and disappeared on the other side of Indian Hill.

I took my daughter's hand and walked over to where they stood. "Hi, Mike. What's it look like?"

I glanced inside the garage. What I saw was worse than I had imagined. Not only were the boxes pulled off the shelves, they'd been upended and the contents scattered. A mental picture of Madge encountering the thief caused me to bite my lip. It could have been disastrous, likely resulting in her getting injured. The back door to her garage was in line with her patio's sliding glass door. It was only about a dozen steps from her bedroom.

"He came prepared," Mike said. "The glass was cut, not broken."

"Someone with experience," I said.

He nodded. "I'd say so."

His partner closed his evidence collecting kit, picked it up and approached. "I haven't picked up any prints," he said, "not even a fragment. He was probably wearing gloves."

Mike pulled a business card out of his pocket and handed it to Madge. "Don't hesitate to call when you figure out what's missing. But frankly," he nodded toward the interior of the garage, "I don't know how you'll be able to tell."

"Thank you for coming so quickly," she said.

"Anytime." With a quick nod to each of us, the two of them headed back to the cruiser.

As soon as they drove away, Madge said, "I'm going to change into some work clothes. I must look a fright. I'd better call Golden Hills Care Home too. The residents will be so disappointed that Wilbur and I can't make our usual scheduled visit. We'll just have to postpone it a day." She turned and headed for the patio door.

I let Jeff out of the car, then ventured into the garage to size up the work ahead. Wilbur followed me, sniffed at some of the papers, sneezing a couple of times. Jeff joined him, wandering through a jumble of folders, binders and photos. Several times, he looked up at me. He'd picked up the scent of a stranger.

I was contemplating where to begin the cleanup when, like a quick-change artist, Madge returned, dressed in denims and matching shirt with the sleeves rolled up.

She grabbed Peggy Lou's hand before my daughter could follow me inside. "Peggy, dear. Why don't you coax the dogs into the backyard and keep them out of the way. They like to play ball." She patted Peggy on the back. "That's a good girl."

I turned over the first box. "What alerted you to the burglar?"

"Wilbur. He started barking. It woke me. I got up to see what had disturbed him. When I looked out the patio door and saw the side door open, I rushed back to put on a robe before going to investigate. I was thinking I'd forgotten to lock it, and some animal, maybe a dog, had pushed the door open. But when I saw the glass was missing from the window…."

"Madge. Who knew these records were stored here?

"Only the members of our chapter."

"Was there anything that could have been recycled for cash?"

Madge shook her head. "Hardly." She picked up a folder and some papers.

Over the next three hours, despite numerous interruptions by Peggy Lou, Madge and I righted all twenty boxes and tried to restore order. With some effort and the help of a ladder, we got them back on the shelves. When we finished, Madge said, "Come on inside. Let's get cleaned up. I feel like a virtual dust mop." She called Peggy, and we all, including the dogs, trooped into the house.

By the time I'd washed up and helped Peggy Lou wash her hands, I could smell the aroma of Madge's favorite blend of coffee. "I don't imagine you had breakfast," she said when we came into view. She set a mug of coffee on the counter that separated the kitchen from the dining room.

"We were in too big a hurry," I said. I helped my daughter scramble into her highchair. "Peggy had a granola bar, and I gave her a package of sliced apples I had in the car." Of course, she'd shared them with the dogs. They think anything she's eating must be good. But I didn't mention that to Madge.

"Hardly a suitable breakfast for a child. I'll prepare a bowl of oatmeal for her." She opened one of her cabinets and took down a box. I recognized the label. It was the same brand of oatmeal she'd made for me when I stayed with her as a child. She always insisted on a healthy breakfast. I grew to hate oatmeal, though I never told her.

I took a seat on one of the counter stools, claimed the mug of coffee and took a sip. Jeff flopped at my feet with Wilbur nearby. "I think Jeff should stay with you again. Having a dog with a loud bark might be the best deterrent, in case the burglar returns."

Madge looked at me with a thoughtful expression, then nodded. "Wilbur is a good watch dog, but I admit he's not nearly as intimidating as your Doberman." She leaned over and opened one of the lower cabinets. A sack rustled. The dogs jumped to their feet and scampered to her side, their toenails making skittering noises on the slick flooring. I couldn't see what she had in her hand, but I could guess.

She walked to the washroom door and opened it. "In you go," she said in a firm, no-nonsense tone. As they obeyed, she gave each of them a dog biscuit. "Good boys," she said, and closing the door, returned her attention to preparing what turned out to be brunch. I soon was treated to a waffle, scrambled eggs and bacon. She served Peggy the bowl of cereal she'd prepared, and joined me at the counter with her share of the meal.

I was still wrestling with the motive behind the invasion of Madge's garage. "Is it remotely possible someone in your ladies' club could have a secret hidden in those files?" I asked, taking a bite of bacon.

"Why? You think she'd break in to steal it?" Madge shook her head. "If that were the case, she would have done it long ago. And besides, there'd be no need to scatter records all over the garage floor. She'd know exactly where to find it. No. Whoever got into my garage was looking for something else, probably something to sell or hock."

I cut a piece of waffle and put it into my mouth, enjoying the taste of the authentic maple syrup Madge buys.

"It's unlikely he'll return, since whoever it was didn't find what they expected." She heaved a sigh. "It's a crazy world we live in, but everything's back where it belongs, and I'll have your big dog staying with me, so I feel safe enough."

I couldn't erase my concern so easily. Not knowing the reason behind the crime left me with a niggling itch. It didn't have the earmarks of a novice thief. As I ate, I reviewed the details I'd observed. I was so focused on my mental meanderings, I hardly noticed when Madge slipped away from her place and began extolling the virtues of cooked cereal to Peggy. I missed half of what she was saying. Minutes later, when the name of Vivian penetrated, I realized she was talking to me.

"I hardly recognized her," she said, expanding on an account of her lunch with Vivian Rudd the previous day. "She is so thin, and it's no wonder. She ordered the smallest lunch selection she could find on the menu, a dinner salad and a cup of soup, which she barely touched. She tasted the soup, pushed it aside and spent the rest of our time together picking at the salad, consuming barely a third of it." In Madge's view, wasting food should be treated as a criminal offense.

"I ordered a nice quiche," she continued, "and would have enjoyed it if it hadn't been for watching her odd behavior."

"I take it that your idea of a pleasant lunch with an old friend didn't turn out that way."

"The change in her amazed me," Madge said. "She used to have a sweet personality, just what children with special needs require. Now... I don't know how I'd class her."

"Did you invite her to join the Women of Colonial Heritage?" I asked before shoveling a forkful of scrambled eggs into my mouth.

"No. I changed my mind about that, because the whole luncheon was just odd. It's the only way I can describe it. When I asked how the family was adjusting to her brother's death, she started complaining about how her younger brother, Will, was being pushed aside by her nephew, Fillmore, and that they're constantly quarrelling. She said that Will, she sometimes calls him Willard, should be the head of the family business now."

"Mmm, yes. I've heard about the power struggle going on."

"The most curious thing was that she talked in circles part of the time. Sometimes I wasn't sure if she was talking about Fillmore, his father or *her* father. She denigrated Claudine's art career, thinks she should help with the office work. It sounds like Tony Grimes' death has brought all the old conflicts bubbling to the surface. It seems like she resented Tony most of their lives, and the fact that he moved "that woman," as she referred to his consort, into his house only added to her angst.

"She got so agitated, her hands were shaking. I tried to change the subject and asked her about her decision to retire. She told me she had no heart for teaching after her husband, Leonard, died four years ago. She lost all desire to live. She even contemplated suicide. I was aghast to say the least. I had to control my inclination to tell her God's view of such things."

"What dissuaded her?"

"She said she decided her younger brother, that's Will, needed her support. She said Tony's attitude toward Will was just like their father's, that Will was a weak little man, too hot headed to run the big business their father had built."

"Is he married?"

"I guess not. She didn't mention a wife."

"Does he have children?"

"No. And that's another thing. Tony wanted the business to pass to the next generation. That meant Fillmore. She didn't think it was fair. And all of it has been made worse by Tony Grimes' death."

"I imagine there'll be lawsuits and counter suits before it's over." I slipped off the stool, took my plate to the kitchen sink, and glanced at the kitchen clock. "But right now, I have some work waiting for me at the office. Thanks so much for brunch." I glanced at Peggy Lou who'd eaten most of her cereal and was stirring the remainder around in the bowl. "I want to get finished and head home early." I walked over and kissed my daughter's cheek before leaving.

Out in the Explorer, I wondered if I was making a mistake leaving Peggy with Madge. But she was probably right. No burglar would return to the scene of the crime the same day, and certainly not in broad daylight.

The whole incident was still bothering me when I parked at the office. I pulled my purse strap onto my shoulder while making grumbling noises to myself about lugging the handgun around with me. I figured I'd end up stoop-shouldered before my time.

I stepped out of the car and was fishing for the office key when my cell phone jingled. I answered, and after a shotgun greeting, Fillmore Grimes said, "Could you come out to the headquarters? We have a situation here."

In the background I heard Claudine's voice saying something I couldn't distinguish. "Okay. Okay," he said, his voice distant, then clear to me. "Claudine wants you to know we'll pay for your time."

Always helpful to know, I thought. "I guess I could be there in about twenty minutes, but what's the nature of your *situation*?"

A muffled back and forth, and then Claudine's voice came on the line. "Oh, Deena. Uncle Will has disappeared."

CHAPTER 28

I arrived at the Grimes' offices in time to see Holly, their receptionist, open the door of a blue Volkswagen Beetle and throw her purse into the passenger seat.

"Holly," I called as I hopped out of the SUV and walked around the front. "What's going on?"

She swung around to face me, her eyelids red-rimmed. "You told me to tell the truth, and now look what's happened!" She slid into the driver's seat, slammed the door and started the engine.

I took a couple of quick steps in her direction in hopes of stopping her. She shot me a venomous glare and mouthed something through the driver's side window as she backed out of the parking space. Without hesitation, she shifted, gears grinding, and turned down the driveway to the main road, spewing a cloud of dust out from under the wheels. I could only guess that her honesty wasn't appreciated by her employer and she blamed me.

I turned toward the entrance, but paused when I noticed a white van parked at the east end of the building. The Sheriff's Department logo was visible on the side panel. A dark-haired man in white coveralls was in the process of loading cardboard boxes from a cart through the back doors. Behind him, a deputy sheriff in a tan uniform held a laptop computer in each arm, the cords dangling from his hand. As soon as the objects were inside, they closed the doors and proceeded to climb into the seats in front, apparently ready to leave.

I made my way through the main entrance into the building, went past the empty reception desk to the passageway where I'd gone to find Fillmore's office the week before. A jumble of voices could be heard coming from the open room at the far end of the hall.

"You mean I've come all this way for nothing?"

A deep male voice, one I didn't recognize.

"Please, don't quarrel," a woman's voice insisted.

"It's your fault!" Claudine's voice, shrill, unlike anything I'd heard from her before.

"My fault! I didn't tell her to spill her guts to those investigators!" Fillmore.

I approached until I stood in the doorway. The room stretched the width of the building with a row of five-by-five windows to the left and right, letting light fill the space. Fillmore and Claudine were standing on either side of an eight-foot oak conference table, bent forward, leaning on it, glaring at each other. Vivian Rudd, seated at the head of the table with her face as pale as freshwater pearls, was staring at them. Two other people, a young man I didn't recognize, and a woman I remembered seeing at Claudine's art show, were also seated there.

The room fairly sparkled with high-voltage emotions. I remained where I was until Claudine noticed my presence. Her flushed face and fierce eyes morphed into a more normal expression. She put her hand on her chest and took a deep breath. Fillmore turned toward me with a jerk, his fury simmering in his cheeks.

Claudine pushed aside the chair behind her and walked around the table in my direction. "I'm glad you could come so quickly." She put her hand on my shoulder and gestured toward the people at the table. "Most of the family is here today. You've met my Aunt Vivian. And this is Dexter Rudd, my cousin." She indicated the man seated next to her aunt, then nodding to direct my attention to the younger woman, she said, "I think you've met Torie, Fillie's wife."

I smiled and nodded to each of them in greeting, noticing a thin stack of papers on the table in front of each chair, even the empty ones. Vivian's son responded with a quick bob of his head, his sour expression unchanged. I guessed him to be in his forties, his hairline in front receding a bit. His square face was not flattered by the dark-rimmed glasses he wore.

Fillmore's wife, a petite blonde dressed in blue jeans and polo shirt, turned in her chair to give me a quick nod and half-hearted smile.

"We had a meeting scheduled for this morning," Claudine continued, "but Uncle Will never arrived. And we can't get a hold of him. We're so worried."

Fillmore grunted. "Worried. I wouldn't put it that way. It seems the authorities think he's absconded with money from the business—the rat." He clinched his fists. "If I could get my hands on him, I'd wring his fat little neck."

A sharp gasp came from Torie.

Vivian spoke up, her voice scratchy, like she might have been crying before I came in. "Stop this! Just stop it! Something's happened to him. I know my brother. This meeting was too important to miss."

I ambled to an empty chair at the other end of the conference table. I wanted a good view of everyone's face. "What makes you think something bad has happened to him?" I extracted a notebook and pen from my purse, laid them on the table and took a seat.

At that moment Rick Morales, Claudine's husband, appeared in the same doorway I'd entered. "Hey, sorry I'm late," he said, stepping forward, the sunlight reflecting off his Calvin Klein suit. "I had to meet a client to sign some papers. Just closed on the sale of that mansion west of Pelterville. What's going on? Why are you all looking so glum? Have you already voted?"

Claudine glared at him. "Not that you'd care, but Uncle Will didn't show, and the sheriff's detectives just left with a pile of financial records."

Rick gave a whistle, walked over to the table, and pulled out a chair. A smirk played on his lips. He sat and ran his fingers across the side of his neck. "You mean like there's been a weasel in the hen house?"

"Oh, shut up," Claudine said. She went back to her place and leaned her hands on the back of the chair. For a second, I wondered if she'd throw it at him.

I flipped open my tablet to a fresh page. "Who spoke to him last, and where was he at the time?"

Fillmore tugged his chair forward to sit. "He didn't come to the office yesterday, but I didn't think much about it."

Claudine turned and focused on Vivian. "You talk to him almost every day, so it must have been you. Where was he?"

"Well...ah...I think he was at home. He called last night." She put an index finger on her lips and turned her head toward the windows as if trying to think of what she could add. "There was noise in the background. I guess he might have been in a restaurant."

"Or bar," Fillmore filled in.

Claudine snorted. "You got no room to talk."

Fillmore's jaw worked. "At least I don't hang out in bars."

"No. You drink alone like a hermit." Claudine turned her attention to me. "I called his house before we called you. There was no answer. I tried his cell number, but it went to voice mail."

"Good God," Morales said. "He can't be that hard to find."

I glanced around the table. "I can check at his home and the places he frequents, if you wish, but I imagine you'll hear from him sometime today. If not, and he doesn't contact any of you, you should call the local police."

Claudine spoke up. "But they won't consider him missing for at least 72 hours."

"We can't wait that long," Vivian chipped in.

I nodded. "All right, then. How about you just tell me the places he frequents and the names of his friends."

Over the next couple of minutes, Fillmore and Claudine suggested people their uncle knew, plus the location of his home and his favorite restaurant. I scribbled as fast as I could, stopping them at times to clarify spelling. Vivian sat silent throughout. She stared at her age-spotted hands, lacing and unlacing her fingers. I was too busy writing to assess what was going on in her mind. When I finished, I looked up at her to see if she had anything to add. She responded with a barely perceptible shake of her head.

Rick Morales scooted his chair back and stood. "If you folks don't need me, I'm going to beat it. I've got people to see and calls to make."

Claudine gave him a dismissive wave, and he left the way he'd come in.

I turned my attention to Fillmore. "Now tell me what the investigators told you."

"Damn little, except that they had information they needed to follow up on. The big dude with the bald head handed over a search warrant. I don't know how I'm supposed to run a business without computer access." He slammed the flat of his hand on the table. "Can't even communicate with the bank."

"Call your attorney," I said. "He can help you make arrangements. Let me see the warrant."

Fillmore leaned forward, reached to pull a folded paper from his back pocket, passed it to me and settled again. I took a minute to read it, noting it listed only financial records. "Which bank branch did your company use?"

"The one in Pelterville."

I returned the warrant to him. "I saw Holly leaving when I arrived. She acted upset."

Fillmore blew air from puffed cheeks. "Dang kid. She admitted she told the investigators she heard my dad and Uncle Willie arguing about money the morning before the plane crash. They were always arguing. There was nothing new about that. But it was all the investigators needed." The crease in his forehead deepened. He leaned forward, braced his elbows on the table and rubbed his eyes with his fingertips. "I canned her."

Claudine, still standing, glared at her brother and propped a fist on her hip. "You shouldn't have done that. She's a good girl, and needs the money to help support her family."

"Well, hell. I don't know how I'd pay her anyway with the financial records gone. No telling when we'll get all this mess straightened out." He looked over at me. "Find the little bastard. Make him tell the police what he's done."

I closed the notebook and returned it and the pen to my bag. "I'll need a recent photo of him."

"There's probably one in his office," Fillmore said. He got to his feet. "I'll check." He went back into the hallway and returned a moment later with a framed photo in his hand. Forcing the backing off, he pulled out a five-by-seven picture of Willard Grimes standing in front of a canary yellow sports car and passed it to me. He pointed at the picture. "He's proud of that car. Cost him a bundle. Treats it like a champion race horse."

Claudine walked to where Vivian was seated. "I'll walk you home, Viv."

"No need. I'm not feeble." Vivian pushed herself out of the chair. "Come on, Dexter. I'll make lunch."

"I don't have time, Mother. I need to get back to Sacramento." He stood and followed her to the double doors at the end of the room. Vivian paused and looked back at me, a question in her eyes.

"I'll be in touch as soon as I have something to report," I said.

She nodded and stepped out, the lines in her face making her look like she'd aged ten years since the art show at Claudine's gallery. The two of them walked toward the two-story green house a few hundred yards away.

"Is that the original family home?" I asked.

Claudine answered. "Yes. She's lived there by herself ever since Uncle Leonard died."

"It's a firetrap," Fillmore muttered.

Claudine touched her forehead, gave a quick head shake and rolled her eyes heavenward. With a glance toward me, she said, "I'm parked out back." She went out the same door as the others, and a moment later, a car door opened and closed. An engine started.

I tucked the photo in my purse, stood and slung the strap over my shoulder.

Fillmore held up his hand, a delaying motion. "Be careful when you locate Uncle Willie. He might be dangerous." He stuffed his hands in his pockets and looked at the floor. "Holly wasn't the only one who overheard Dad and Uncle Willie the day of the crash. It didn't register at the time, but now I think Dad probably figured out Willie was cooking the books. I hate to think it, but ...." He looked up at me, his eyes reflecting a painful speculation, as if saying it out loud could make it real.

CHAPTER 29

I understood where Fillmore was going with his idea. It might have seemed logical on the surface, but I wasn't ready to jump to the same conclusion. "When did *you* see him last?"

"The other night at Claudine's gallery. He had his shorts in a twist because I'd moved into Dad's office. That's why it's so odd his not showing up here this morning. He was aching for a fight over control of the business."

"You think he knew about the search warrant?"

"I don't see how. I got here before eight. The detective with the papers arrived soon afterward. Then Claudine, Aunt Viv, and the others came in a little before nine." Drawing his hand across the back of his neck, he stared out the window for a moment. "Unless…he drove in, saw the Sherriff's van and left without being noticed."

"I doubt he's gone very far. I'll do some quick checking around. Do you happen to know the license number on his car?"

"I don't. It's one of those vanity plates. He drove a company pickup most of the time. He said it was too dirty around here to bring his car out. I think he bought the sports car because he figured it would attract women."

I had a hard time keeping a straight face, remembering his uncle's thick glasses and thinning gray hair. But on second thought his uncle might have been right. That sports car *would* attract attention, as would his notoriety as part of a successful farming corporation.

"The photo will be sufficient for now," I said. "I have a ready source for that sort of information. I take it he's not married."

Fillmore smiled and shook his head. "Actually, he's had three wives. The last one lasted three months. I'm not sure, but I suspect he might have popped her one, and she decided she didn't sign up for that."

He motioned to Torie, who'd had little to say during the whole meeting. She stood, placed her handbag on the table, reached in and extracted a pen and slip of paper. The purse was a Gucci, a CG pendent dangling from the strap. It spoke of money, as did her shoes and Burberry shirt. Laying the paper on the table, she wrote a single word on it, then turned and handed it to me. "You might check there," she said. "It's a nightclub located north of Pelterville on what used to be the main highway before the new one went in."

I read the name out loud. "The Hideaway."

Fillmore's eyebrows raised. "How come *you* know

where he hangs out?"

She tilted her head to give him a sideways look and folded her arms across her chest. "Before he left Claudine's gallery the other night, I overheard him apologize to Vivian and Claudine for leaving early. He told Viv he couldn't stand the sight of you any longer and indicated that that," she pointed to the paper, "was where he was going. I doubt Claudine heard. She had her eyes fixed on Bobbie Castro."

"Why didn't you bring it up before now?" Fillmore asked.

She dropped the pen back into her handbag and closed it before speaking. "Two reasons. I didn't want to embarrass your aunt, and...I didn't want to admit I'd been eavesdropping."

Fillmore grinned and shook his head.

I smiled. "Maybe I should hire you."

Torie swiped a lock of her shoulder-length hair over her ear. "Keeping track of our three boys is enough job for me." She smiled up at Fillmore. "And taking care of the big guy."

He put his arm around her shoulder and gave her an affectionate squeeze, then turned his attention to me. "I guess I better call Cliff Jessup and see what can be done about getting around the mess Willie's created. I wish I could be more help, but as soon as I talk to Cliff, I've got to fly to Phoenix and meet Reed Monroe, our ranch manager over there. I haven't talked to him since the funeral. Dad always said staying in contact with employees is the difference between making and losing money. I'll drive past Uncle Willie's house and check to see if his car is there. If it is, I'll let you know."

"Don't approach him. Like you said, he might be unpredictable."

"Oh, I won't. We live just a quarter mile down the road from his place. Dad's house is first in line, then Uncle Willie's, then ours. We each have an acre with a walnut grove in between," he grinned, "to keep us from fighting." He reached for Torie's hand. "I wish Aunt Viv had built a new home down there next to mine. I hate to see her living by herself in the old house. Even though she keeps it maintained, I'm not sure it's safe. Old wiring, you know."

Torie spoke up. "Why Fill, she loves the old place. And so do I." She turned to me. "You should see it during the holidays. The way she has it decorated, it's like a Currier and Ives come to life. She invites the whole family for holiday dinners." She looked at her husband. "The boys wouldn't think it was Christmas if we didn't go there."

Fillmore stuck out his hand to me. "Call my cell anytime."

We shook hands, and I departed, leaving the same way I'd entered the building.

Out in the parking lot, I'd just snapped the seat belt when Fillmore burst out the door waving a sheet of paper. He rushed to my driver's side window.

The first thing that popped into my head was—suicide note. I lowered the window and leaned out.

"I found this on my desk," he said, holding the paper out to me.

I took it and studied the scrawl. It looked like it had been written with a felt pen.

The message said, *"I didn't do it!"*

"That's Uncle Willie's handwriting," Fillmore said. "He must have come inside after I left my office to set up for the meeting."

I shrugged and handed the paper back to him. "What do you think he means?"

"Hard to tell for sure, but it proves he was here. I'm sure he saw the sheriff's van."

"Seems like it. I'll be in touch." I started the SUV and backed out.

As I drove away, I glanced in the rear view mirror. Fillmore was still standing by the door staring at the paper in his hand. It was easy to tell his emotions had swung from anger to frustration to worry. I was a little worried too. A man like Willard Grimes, a man with a temper, pushed into a corner, could act out in unspeakable ways. I wondered if he knew Fillmore was about to fly to Arizona.

CHAPTER 30

I took an alternate route back to Four Creeks, the one that would take me past The Hideaway where Will Grimes liked to spend time. The two-lane road ran along the lower edge of a steep hill, one where a couple of expensive-looking homes clung to the upper perimeter.

Farther along, I found what I was looking for on the left, on the downhill side of the road. The Hideaway was a squatty building, made of dark wood to give it an old west appeal. But the neon sign on the front was anything but *old west*, and by the size of it, seclusion was not their intention. I could only imagine what it looked like at night.

Two cars were parked in front, but Grimes' sports car was not one of them. I turned in with the thought of finding a friend of his who might have an idea of where to look for him. I glided to a stop near the entrance. With my purse and the photo of Will Grimes, I got out and made my way to the wide-wooden door.

Just inside, I stepped to my right, out of the doorway, and paused to allow my eyes to adjust to the change in light. A counter directly ahead held all the common accoutrements one might expect—a stack of menus, a register and several impulse items. Since it was still early afternoon, I doubted I'd see many patrons. But I was surprised when I didn't see or hear anyone at all, though I did hear music coming from an audio system. It sounded like one of the oldies from the 70s.

A glance to my right revealed a dining room with a dozen round tables, each covered with a white tablecloth and set with table service. No diners.

In the other direction, I saw a dance floor the size of our living room at home. On the far side, a space suitable for a small band was surrounded by café tables. I ventured through the open doorway and noticed two men, one gray-haired, the other bald, perched on stools at the far end of a thirty-foot bar. They had their backs to me and were in a quiet conversation, one expressing himself with his hands. A TV over the bar had a sports channel running.

The clink of glass-on-glass drew my attention to a woman with henna-red curls piled on top of her head. She was arranging clean glasses on a counter behind the bar. She was wearing a sleeveless shirt, which allowed a partial view of a large blue butterfly tattoo on each of her substantial biceps.

"Excuse me," I said to get her attention, since she was facing away from me. She swung around, gave me a quick once-over and smiled. "Have a seat. What'll you have?"

She was not young. I placed her age at past fifty. I slid onto a stool opposite her, produced my I.D. and introduced myself. "I hope you can help me," I said, laying the photo of Grimes on the bar's surface. "I'm looking for this man. His family is very concerned because they can't seem to locate him." I paused, watching her reaction.

She leaned an elbow on the bar and stared at the photo. "I might have seen someone who sort of looks like him." She straightened. "But that must be an old picture. The guy I'm thinking of doesn't have that much hair and wears thick glasses."

"What about the car?" I asked, pointing to it.

"Oh, honey, when it's busy in here, I don't have time to go out and check the parking lot." She turned to her right. "Hey, Joe," she called out—loud enough to cause the two men to swivel and stare at us. "Come take a look at this picture."

Both men rose and walked over to where I sat. She pushed the photo toward them. "You think this looks like the fellow that comes in here on weekends?"

The bald guy, I assumed was Joe, picked up the photo, held it at eye level and squinted at it. He needed the glasses in his shirt pocket. "Sure. That's Will. That's his car too." He looked at me. "Has something happened to him?"

"This here's a private detective," the lady barkeeper said. "She's looking for him 'cause his family can't find 'im."

"Do you remember when he was in here last?" I asked.

Joe rubbed his chin. "Well, I'd say last weekend." He turned to the other man. "What do you say, Pete?" He handed the picture to him.

"Yup," Pete said after a glance at the photo. "Saturday night. There was a good crowd, and I wouldn't have noticed except he got into an argument with another guy. I thought for a second he was going to punch him out, but he left instead."

"You haven't seen him since?" I asked.

All three shook their heads. I thanked them all around, retrieved the photo and departed. The only thing I'd established was that Willard Grimes had gone there the night of the gallery showing.

Out in the Explorer, I was ready to pull out onto the road again when my cell phone alerted me to a call. It was Fillmore Grimes.

"I stopped at George Taylor's place across from Uncle Willie's," he said. "Asked if he'd noticed whether my uncle had been back to his house since this morning. He said he'd gone fishing and had just returned home. There was no sign of Uncle Willie at the house. His truck is parked in its usual spot. The garage door was closed, so I drove into the yard and looked through the garage window. His car wasn't there. I'm just about to take off, so I'll be out of touch for a few hours. I'll call after I land at the Arizona ranch."

I said thanks and the call ended.

During the drive to the office, I mulled over what could have motivated Willard Grimes to pull a vanishing act. If the only thing he'd done was to misappropriate monies from the corporation, his hiding out seemed a bit of overkill. His reason would play a big part in locating him. Vivian's concern that something bad had happened to him seemed over-the-top too. And what did he mean by his note. Fillmore's unspoken suspicion kept edging into my thoughts.

As soon as I got to the office, I called the local hospitals and learned that no one by that name had been admitted. Then I called Buzz, gave him the lowdown on the turmoil going on in the Grimes family and asked him to check for the license number of Willard or Will Grimes' car.

"Technically, I shouldn't do that," he said, "but since you're family, I guess I can bend the rules. Right now, I'm on the prowl for a thief who stole a kid's bike out of the school's bike rack. I'll get back to you as soon as I can."

While I waited to hear from him, I decided to see if I could dredge up more info on the elusive Will Grimes. With the list the family had supplied and using the internet, over the next fifteen minutes, I learned more about him than he might have imagined. No life is safe from cyber intrusion. Beyond the usual profile, his not-infrequent bouts of temper had caused his name to show up in the local newspaper every few years. He'd used the company truck as a battering ram on one occasion when someone locked a gate to land he wanted access to, and another time, he decked a guy for insulting his wife.

His divorces turned out to be of interest too. He'd been married to Gwendolyn Fisher for ten years, Joann Bailey for four, and his last marriage, to Deanna Schultz, lasted six months. To dig into court records would take too much time at the moment, but I suspected Uncle Will needed anger control counseling.

The jingle of my cell phone alerted me to Buzz's return call.

"I've got it," he said, and reeled off the numbers and letters for the sports car, along with the vin number, which I added to my list. "Good luck," he said. "Be careful."

"Thanks, honey. I'm hoping he's just spooked, and not really planning to leave town. If I can find him, I'll try to convince him that the best thing would be to contact his attorney and abide by his counsel."

Buzz concurred. "That would be good advice. It sounds like he's gone off half-cocked. It could be days before the detectives will know whether or not there's been any wrong-doing with the company's accounts."

The door to the office building opened and Bert entered. She had a packet of mail in her hand and was wearing black slacks and a long-sleeved sequined blouse. I waved to her. "I'll fill you in on what I learn tonight," I said to Buzz and ended the call.

I pushed out of my desk chair and took the picture of Willard Grimes and his expensive sports car to show her. Light from the window made Bert's sequins sparkle. "Nice blouse. New?"

"Yup. Found it on a close-out rack at Macy's. Kinda goes along with my boots." She laid the mail on her desk, tilted her leg and hiked up her pant leg to expose a streak of glitter on the side of her boot. "Classy, huh?"

"Sure, why not."

Brushing her pant leg down, she sat at her desk and picked up a notepaper. "A man by the name of Russ Treadwell called a little while ago. Said he had something he wanted you to do for one of his clients. You want me to get him on the phone for you?"

"That will have to wait. I have something more pressing right now." I handed her the photo. "Scan this and make a few copies. I need you to drive over to Delta and check out the major hotels."

"Sounds interesting. Who am I looking for?"

I pointed to the picture. "His name is Willard Grimes, Uncle Will to Claudine and Fillmore. He didn't show up for an important meeting this morning, and his family are frantic to find him. Though they wouldn't come right out and say it, I think they're afraid he might harm himself."

CHAPTER 31

While Bert went off to scour hotel parking lots for Will Grimes' car, I settled at my desk and pulled out the local phone directory to look up the number for Marvin Stuart, the entomologist Fillmore had mentioned as one of his uncle's friends.

When I called, he wasn't in. His message service indicated a cell phone number, so I gave it a try. He answered on the third ring, his voice deep like a radio or TV announcer, prompting a mental picture of a man with a barrel chest and a thick neck.

I identified myself and explained the reason for my inquiry, but he said he hadn't heard from Grimes since they'd had coffee the week before.

"Any thoughts on where I might find him?"

"I don't, and I can't imagine how he would forget a meeting like that one." He paused and I was about to break in with another question, when he said, "Come to think of it, last time I saw him, he did act sort of...I guess I'd call it distracted. I didn't give it much thought. This is my busiest time of year, so I'm sorta distracted myself these days. I see him at this wine tasting club we belong to, but last Friday when the group got together, Will couldn't come, said he had to help his niece prepare for a showing of her art work at her gallery."

"Does he have a girlfriend?" A man with secrets might keep that sort of personal relationship from his family, especially if he'd been married three times already.

"If he does, he never mentioned one to me."

I thanked Mr. Stuart for his time, recited my contact numbers, and asked him to call if he thought of something that would help. He said he would, and our conversation ended.

I leaned back in my chair and considered Grimes' situation. He wasn't at home, he avoided his usual contacts, and as far as his friend knew, there was no girlfriend in the picture where he would hide out.

A man's gotta eat, I reasoned. A glance at my list told me he favored Chinese food. I grabbed my purse, locked up, and headed for The Golden Wok. It was local, a guess at best, but worth a try.

I got lucky with parking and hustled to pull open the door. As soon as I entered, the blended aroma of Chinese cuisine stimulated my appetite. A woman's gotta eat too.

A dark-haired woman behind the cash register nodded to me as she finished settling a customer's bill. I took a menu from the counter and was ready when she was free. I ordered pork chow mein, then showed her

Grimes' picture and asked if she seen him that day. She scowled at it and shook her head.

There were probably a half-dozen Chinese restaurants between Four Creeks and the Grimes headquarters. If I were going to check them all, it would take the rest of the afternoon.

I took my order back to the office and had just finished eating when Fillmore called from Arizona. I had to confess I had nothing much to report.

"Try his ex-wife," he said. "Her name's Deanna Shultz. She's a manicurist there in Four Creeks. If he's really desperate, he might get in touch with her."

I was feeling a little desperate, myself. In a search like this one, the first few hours are the most important. "Wasn't their divorce rather acrimonious?"

"It sure was, but he might figure, you know, any old port in a storm." Over some background noise, he said. "Claudine just called me. She says Aunt Viv is coming unraveled. I don't know what she thinks I can do about it. I won't be able to get home till late tomorrow. If you can't locate Uncle Willie by that time, we'll have to contact the police, no matter what Aunt Viv says."

I told him I'd keep searching, disconnected and turned to the computer. An ex-wife might know more about my subject than his family. A few ex-wives I'd met in the past were happy to share their husband's secrets. The search engine indicated there were three hair salons in town. Style Expressions caught my eye. It was the one Aunt Madge patronized. Though I couldn't be sure it was the correct one, I locked up again and took a chance. Aunt Madge had said it was the most popular in town, and that she often had a hard time getting an appointment when she wanted one. I reasoned that an ambitious manicurist would want just such a location.

Parking was scarce around Style Expressions, and I had to settle for a space across the street. I made a dash to the entrance and pulled open the door. As before, the odors of shampoo, hair dye, and nail polish assaulted my senses. When I didn't find anyone minding the counter, I moved through the arched doorway into the working part of the establishment.

The room's arrangement hadn't changed since the time when I'd accompanied Madge to get her hair done before the Whelan funeral. Three elderly ladies sat under whirring hairdryers. A couple of hair stylists chatted with clients while they worked. A manicurist with purple-streaked hair was focused on the hands of the woman seated before her.

"Excuse me for interrupting," I said. "I'm looking for Deanna."

The manicurist looked up at me. It was hard to miss the purple eye shadow and enhanced eyelashes accentuating her dark eyes. "In the john," she said.

"She'll be back in a minute. Have a seat." She motioned to a cushioned bench.

I was considering her invitation, when a woman about my age emerged from an adjacent hall. She was at least four inches taller than me and slender and walked like a dancer in a fluid motion. It wasn't just her walk that drew my attention, but the jeans she wore. They had ragged areas along her thighs and knees and probably cost her an entire week's pay.

"Hey, Dee. Here's your four o'clock after all," the first manicurist said.

I shook my head. "I didn't have an appointment."

"Well, you're in luck," Deanna said, brushing her long dark hair over her shoulder. "My regular client was a no-show." She walked over to her station, gesturing for me to follow and pulled out the chair for me. "Take a load off."

A manicure would eat up too much of my afternoon. My plan was to simply find out what she knew about Will Grimes and be on my way. "Actually, I just wanted to ask you a couple of questions."

She settled on her stool and gestured for me to sit down at her table. "Okay, but let's have a look at those hands of yours."

I eased down onto the chair and held them out.

She grimaced. "Whoa, what do you *do* for a living?"

I didn't think my nails looked *that* bad. "I'm a private investigator. And I'm trying to locate your ex-husband."

She sniffed. "Which one? I've got three."

"You've got three ex-husbands? Sounds like a string of bad luck."

"More like stupidity on my part. Always was a sucker for blue eyes and a wallet full of green."

"It's Will Grimes, I'm trying to find."

"Oh yeah, him. It was the wallet full of green that attracted me. Boy, what a mistake. He wasn't about to part with any of that money. He acted like every dollar was his last. And besides that, he had no imagination in the bedroom." She reached for a hand towel on a nearby shelf. "Know what I mean? Now Jerry, the guy I'm with now? He takes my breath away."

I wasn't particularly interested in her love life, so I short-circuited her story line. "Have you heard from Grimes in the last couple days?"

"Are you kidding? He wouldn't come near me, not after what happened." She placed the folded towel on the table and reached for my left hand.

I almost pulled back, wondering if the Grimes Corporation would object to the cost of a manicure on my expense report. She must have read my mind.

"Come on, it's not *that* expensive. We might as well do something with those nails."

I relented, and she began filing, snipping, and reshaping my cuticles. Twenty minutes later, I was no closer to finding Will Grimes. I did learn more about their brief marriage. She described in detail how she'd met Will Grimes at The Hideaway a couple of years earlier and married in the flush of passion, much to the horror of his family, especially Vivian.

"His older sister had it in for me from day one," Deanna said as she deftly applied a final coat of pink nail polish. "She'd call his cell phone, and he'd pick up and go, no matter the time of day, or night. And he never would explain her problem. It just blew my mind, the hold she had on him. Once he left me sitting in a restaurant.

"I wanted him to go see a doctor about…" She scowled. "You know." She capped the bottle of polish. "Finally, I'd had enough. We had a big blowup. I accused him of being gay and he hit me. I packed my stuff and filed for divorce. Best thing I ever did, 'cause I met Jerry a month later. Now there's a man with imagination." She looked at me and lifted her sculpted eyebrows. "Know what I mean?"

I decided it was best not to ask for clarification. Instead, I held my hands up and admired my nails. They did look better.

"Give them a little time to dry," she said, "and you'll be good to go. Now that wasn't so bad, was it?" She smiled at me like a mother to a child.

Another ten minutes and I stood at the counter to pay my bill. "So I take it you have no idea where Will Grimes would go if he wanted to elude his family or the authorities?"

Deanna gave me a shocked look. "Authorities? Good God. What'd he do, murder somebody?" With a quick shake of her head, she said, "Gosh, no. I wasn't with him long enough to learn things like that. Sorry."

I handed her my card and asked her to get in touch if she heard from him. She agreed, and I went out onto the sidewalk. I'd struck out again. Back in the Explorer, I decided I'd continue the search the next day. As I maneuvered through late afternoon traffic and up Indian Hill to Madge's house, Claudine called on my cell. I pulled into Madge's driveway and answered.

"Deena, I just don't know what to do," she said in a fretful tone. "Aunt Viv is teetering on the edge of a nervous breakdown. I told her to take a sedative, but she says she must talk to you. Can you go out to her house?"

"Now?"

"Yes. Pleeease."

"I'm sorry. Right now I have to pick up my daughter. It's too late to do anything more today."

There was a five second pause at her end of the line. "I guess you're right," she said, her tone deflated. "Of course you are. We're just so worried about Uncle Will, I doubt any of us will sleep tonight."

CHAPTER 32

Frustration had given me a headache by the time I picked up Peggy Lou at Aunt Madge's and arrived home at the ranch. I'd achieved nothing in my efforts to locate Willard Grimes. Bert had called to say she'd checked all the hotels in the city of Delta and driven by most of the motels in the area, but hadn't seen even one yellow sports car. I'd talked to everyone on the list his family had given me, and no one seemed to have a clue as to where he might be.

For the next hour, I set all that aside to focus on preparing our dinner. When Buzz arrived at six-thirty, he looked more tired than usual, tension apparent in the way he moved. Peggy Lou, busy with wooden puzzles on the living room floor, scrambled to her feet to greet her daddy. He scooped her up in his arms and gave her a kiss, then put her down, unlike his usual playful manner.

"You look beat. Want some coffee?" I asked, reaching for a clean cup in the cupboard.

"Right now, I need a shower." He gave me a peck on the cheek and headed down the hall.

I put our salads on the table, and a half-hour later, Buzz helped Peggy Lou into her highchair, before settling himself in his usual place.

I placed the last of the serving dishes on the table and took a seat. "How was your day?"

He poured a generous portion of ranch dressing on his salad. "Mostly routine patrol, a few traffic stops. Found the stolen bike." He handed the bottle to me, picked up his fork and began to eat.

I put a little dressing on Peggy Lou's kid-sized salad and a blob on my own. I studied him while I ate. By the way he dug into that salad, he had something on his mind. I knew he'd get around to telling me, but I wasn't inclined to wait him out. "Have you heard any rumors about financial fraud at the Grimes Corporation?"

He grabbed a napkin from a stack on the table, wiped his mouth, and set his salad plate aside. "No, but I *have* heard some other news."

"Yeah? What?"

"I had a call from Mike Huerta before I left work." Buzz picked up his fork and looked at me across the table. "You didn't mention the break-in at your aunt's house when you called this afternoon."

"You're right. I planned to tell you about it, but Will Grimes' disappearance was uppermost on my mind right then."

"The break-in could be more significant than you thought." He stabbed a piece of chicken and put it on his plate. "Remember Mike's sister, Maria? She lives over on the south side of Pelterville now. He says she moved over there after Eddie was sentenced to prison."

How could I forget either of them? Eddie Lee had been the one who'd killed Lottie Weston. I had an instant flash of him glaring at me in court, and another of Maria holding her sick baby the day I went to their house looking for him. Even though it had been years, those images were hard to erase.

Buzz added a scoop of mashed potatoes to his plate. "Mike tells me that this afternoon when Maria got home from work, she noticed one of the windows in the house was broken. She got out of her car and was about to examine the damage when she thought she heard someone inside. It scared her, so she called the police."

I listened while I prepared Peggy Lou's dinner plate. It was common for Buzz to recount some harrowing tale of a police chase or parole sweep during dinner. But this was Mike's sister, making it far more compelling.

"When the patrol car arrived," he continued, "the SOB took off out the back door. They chased him between the houses for several blocks. And they would have had him, except when he came to the river where it runs along that side of town, instead of giving up, he plunged in."

223

Buzz had my undivided attention. The thought of it gave me a shiver. Some people do the dumbest things.

"He probably thought if he could get to the far side he'd get away," Buzz went on, tapping the table top with his fork like he does sometimes when describing a tense situation. "Big mistake. That river might not be very wide, but this time of year, coming out of the mountains like it does, it's cold and swift.

"He didn't make it to the other side. The guys saw him float off out of reach. Another patrol car was dispatched to the bridge a mile downstream to wait and haul him out. When he didn't show up, everyone figured he'd been sucked under. They scoured the river bank and surrounding area till dark. No sign of him."

"What a fool," I observed. "He undoubtedly drowned. They'll drag the river tomorrow, won't they?"

Buzz shrugged. "The thing is, Maria got a fairly decent look at the guy. She told the police she thought he looked a lot like Buck Harper. Turns out the officers thought the same thing." Buzz cut the chicken and took a bite.

I flinched as though I'd been jabbed with a knife.

"I was told he tore up Maria's house pretty bad. Scattered stuff all over the place like he was looking for something."

My mind skipped back to the break-in of Madge's garage. "I didn't think the break-in had looked like the work of an amateur, but it hadn't occurred to me that Buck Harper could be the culprit."

Buzz reached for the dish of vegetables. "I think we need to take precautions."

"I don't see how anyone could survive a river that cold."

"Probably not, but humor me. At least until they recover his body."

"What do you have in mind?"

"Besides keeping your handgun at your side at all times, I think your aunt should go stay with a friend." Buzz got out of his chair and went to the refrigerator. He took a bottle of orange juice out and carried it to the table, then took his seat again.

"I doubt she'll agree to that. We spent most of the morning putting the boxes in her garage back in order. She had to skip taking Wilber to Golden Hills Care Home for his weekly visit. She'll insist they have to go tomorrow."

Buzz poured himself a glass of juice. "Well, I'd feel better if you and Peggy Lou stayed home."

"It's unlikely he's still alive. But if he were, he was able to find out where Maria Lee lives, so there's no reason to think he couldn't find out where *we* live. We'd be better off in town around other people."

Buzz shook his head. "I disagree."

"The Grimes family is counting on me to locate Will Grimes. Claudine called and said her Aunt Vivian is so distraught over what's happened that she fears for her health. The woman is asking that I come to her house, and Claudine begged me to go talk to her."

Peggy Lou had been watching our faces. Sensing the tension, she hadn't touched her food.

"Let's finish our dinner," I said in the most cheerful manner I could manage. I took a deep breath and forked a sizable bite of mashed potatoes into my mouth. It took an effort to swallow it past the lump in my throat. Buck Harper hated me with a purple passion. He'd tried to kill me three times, but somehow I couldn't just give in and hide.

When we finished eating, I wiped Peggy Lou's hands with a damp napkin and released her to go play with her toys while Buzz and I cleared the dishes from the table. Wanting to help, Peggy Lou reached for the jar of strawberry jam. It slipped out of her hands and smashed on the floor. Buzz and I turned from the dishwasher. With a whimper, she tried to pick it up, getting jam all over her hands. Afraid she'd cut herself, Buzz rushed over and picked her up. He carried her to the kitchen sink. I got the dust pan and cleaned up the broken glass.

When I returned from depositing the glass in the trash, Buzz was washing her hands, water and jam running down the drain. She had a tiny nick on her thumb from the broken jar and it was bleeding.

The sight of it reminded me of an incident when I was seven and had cut my hand washing dishes. It was during one of the weeks after my mother's funeral. I wanted to be a help to Dad and doing the dishes seemed like the best way. He hadn't smiled in so long, I was afraid he'd never smile again. To me the furrows in his forehead and between his eyes were permanent. It was his worry face, there when he dropped me off at school, and when he picked me up at the end of the day.

I knew why he was troubled. I'd heard my parents talking one night when they thought I was asleep. A few days earlier, one of Dad's coworkers had been killed while trying to apprehend a crook during a liquor store robbery. Because Mom was so sick with the cancer, she worried about what would happen to me if a gunman shot my dad, and she wasn't around to take care of me. It worried me too. I'd read about children who ended up in orphanages, though I didn't know of one in our county.

That summer and all the following summers until we moved to Four Creeks, I stayed with Aunt Madge and Uncle Henry. Dad phoned every evening, and though I was having fun living with them, I waited for those calls like a kid waits for Christmas. I couldn't sleep until I'd talked to him.

Buzz gently wiped Peggy's hand with a paper towel. He handed her off to me and went to get the package of bandages from the bathroom. I sat at the table with her on my lap. The recollection had made me think about the risk of Peggy becoming an orphan. A private investigator's job usually involves nothing more dangerous than background checks, witness location, and process serving. Depending on the case, it could be risky, I knew that, but it was a calculated risk. The idea is to be sure the odds are on your side.

Buzz returned with the smallest of the Band-Aid assortment and applied it to her thumb. She smiled and scooted off my lap, happy to go play with her puzzles.

That night as I settled in my bed, it wasn't Will Grimes' disappearance, or Vivian's impending breakdown that kept me awake. It was the slim possibility that Buck Harper might have somehow escaped from that icy river.

CHAPTER 33

I called Madge as soon as I got up the next morning, told her about Buck Harper's watery escape trick, and that Buzz thought it might have been Harper who broke into her garage. I suggested she spend the day with a friend. As I predicted, she refused to put off visiting the patients at Golden Hills Care Home.

"They have so little to look forward to," she said. "We just can't let them down. And Wilbur would miss all the attention he receives when we're there. If that convict was the person who broke into my garage, he'd have no reason to come back. He didn't find anything he wanted. Your Doberman will be guarding my house, and besides, I have a man from The Glass Emporium coming at one o'clock to replace the broken window in the garage."

I knew it was useless to try to talk her out of her plans, so I didn't try. Either way, Peggy Lou would be with me all day. After that, I called Bert and gave her the day off. When I told her that Buck Harper had made it all the way to Pelterville, she didn't hesitate to accept my offer.

I don't know if I really thought Harper was alive, or not, but after seeing to our breakfast and dressing Peggy Lou, I squirmed into my body holster and slid the PPK into it. It was just as uncomfortable as I remembered. I put on a loose jacket to cover it, checked the spare magazine to be sure it was full, and put it in my purse. With snacks and a bag of things to amuse Peggy Lou, we climbed into the Explorer and headed for town.

I circled the block around the office, and a couple of adjacent blocks as well, checking for anything that would raise my caution meter, such as a vehicle or individual that was out of place. People tend to be creatures of habit, parking, eating, working, and carrying on their lives in the same manner most days. So when someone or something new appears, it's noticeable. We're all aware of those things to one degree or another, but it's the police, and likewise, private investigators, who tend to be more keen observers. Everything in the office neighborhood appeared normal, so I pulled into our parking lot.

Peggy Lou made a bee-line for her "kid's corner" as soon as we were inside the office. With her busy, I settled at my desk, booted up the computer and updated my notes related to my efforts to locate Willard Grimes.

Since no one I'd talked to had seen or heard from him, I reasoned that I should pay a visit to his home. Fillmore might have been wrong. His uncle could be hiding where we wouldn't think to look. If my presence were noticed by his neighbor, I figured Peggy Lou being with me would make it seem like a social call, perhaps a new lady friend. A good plan, I thought. The only other place I considered visiting was Tony Grimes' house. With Bobbie Castro gone, it would be empty. Fillmore had talked about changing the locks, but that wouldn't be much of an impediment for me.

I used an online map website to get a fix on the location of both houses, then pulled my copy of the agreement I had with the Grimes Corporation and made a duplicate to take along. If I were going to be sneaking into houses, I'd better make sure I had a contract to cover my assets, so to speak. Technically, it was no longer valid, but it would be better than going "barefoot" if someone thought I was a burglar and called the police.

I'd also take my carry-all bag. At a minimum, it held items like my camera and special lens, binoculars, a good pocket knife and my micro-tape recorder. I tossed in an extra notebook and pen, then transferred the recorder to my purse along with my lock picks.

I admit it, I was stalling. I wasn't looking forward to visiting Vivian Rudd. Her behavior had me puzzled. She'd struck me as being haughty the night of the art show. But then, beyond wringing her hands, she'd had little to say during the family meeting. Will Grimes was her favorite according to what everyone reported. From his ex-wife's description of how close they were, why didn't she have a better idea of where he might have gone? The whole family was a puzzle with all the animosity that had filtered down through the years. I couldn't understand people like that, but those kinds of problems kept people like me in business. Thinking back on the group dynamics, I sensed I'd missed something. I reviewed my encounters with each person in the family, but couldn't bring anything new to mind.

It had clouded over by the time I put my carry-all bag on the floorboard in front of the passenger seat of the SUV and my purse on the seat. The TV weatherman had predicted rain, but I had doubts about it. Most years, rain was scarce in April.

I walked Peggy Lou around to the passenger side of the car and helped her into her car seat. She dropped her toy kitten three times before I got her buckled in. I brushed off the dirt and handed it to her. She was an active little girl. Being stuck in a car seat all morning was going to be hard for her to tolerate.

My cell phone alerted me to a call. It was Claudine again. I settled in the driver's seat to answer.

"I hope you're going to Aunt Vivian's this morning," she said. "She just called me, said she didn't sleep at all last night, that she'd walked the floor."

"I'm on my way in that direction," I told her, "but there's a couple of places I want to check out first."

Like she hadn't heard what I'd said, she rattled on. "I'd go myself, but my employee called in sick. She's in the ER and may have appendicitis. I'll have to tend the gallery all day. Roz is working. She can't help me. You're the only one free."

"Not exactly. I have my daughter with me today. Does your aunt like children?"

"She was a teacher. Of course, she does."

"Say, Claudine. Who would be the beneficiary of your father's life insurance policy?"

Silence. I waited.

"My mother would have been, but she passed away ten years ago. So I guess it would be Fillie and me. We have an appointment with Cliff this Friday. Why?"

"Just trying to get a better picture of why your Uncle Will might have felt compelled to embezzle." It was a subterfuge. By all indications, *someone* had tampered with Tony Grimes' plane, and I was wondering who had the most to gain. According to what Russ Treadwell had said, there was a double indemnity clause in the policy. However, it wouldn't pay off unless the crash was an accident.

"It breaks my heart to think he did that," she said. "Phone me as soon as you've spoken to Aunt Viv. I hope you can calm her."

I assured her I would try. Our conversation over, I buckled my seat belt and pulled out onto the street.

The drive south to where the Grimes' homes were lined up on Swifter Avenue took a little more than fifteen minutes. I found myself glancing in the rearview mirror. There was no indication that anyone was following. Before long I made the turn onto Swifter and slowed the SUV as I approached where I thought the first of the homes should be. On the north side of the road, I noticed a man with a shovel standing in front of a brown house. I figured he was George Taylor, the man Fillmore had spoken to the day before. There'd be no harm in asking him if he'd seen Will Grimes.

He turned as I pulled into his driveway. I took my identification from my purse, got out of the car and walked over to him. He was no taller than me, with gray hair and glasses.

"Mr. Taylor?"

He nodded, holding the shovel handle like a staff. Dirt on the knees of his jeans was evidence he'd been working in his flower bed.

"I'm Deena Powers," I said, holding up the ID. "I'm looking into a matter for the Grimes family. I was wondering if you'd seen Mr. Will Grimes drive by since yesterday."

"That's the same thing young Fillmore asked me. I haven't been watching the road. I've got this galdarned gopher tearing up the roots of my Lady Washington rose bush." He looked down at a pile of dirt at his feet. "It'll sure kill it, if I don't do something quick."

Not being a gardener, I didn't know what to say, so I mumbled something to sound sympathetic.

He looked up at me. "The last time I talked to Will Grimes was the day after his older brother was killed. I drove down to tell him how sorry I was to hear it. He didn't seem too broken up about what happened. Odd fellow. What's going on? Is he lost or something?"

I explained one more time why I was looking for Grimes.

He rubbed his nose with the back of his hand. "Well, I've been out here since breakfast. I haven't seen him, and it's darn hard to miss that yellow car of his."

I thanked Mr. Taylor, returned to the Explorer and climbed in.

"Me hungee," Peggy Lou said, reaching for the paper bag she knew contained a snack. I turned in my seat and felt the holster rub against my rib cage. With a quick prayer that the police would find Buck Harper's body that day, I grabbed the bag and ripped open the little plastic package of sliced apples I'd brought along. After handing her a piece, I backed out of Mr. Taylor's driveway and steered the car onto the road heading west.

A sprawling ranch house soon came into view. From what Fillmore had told me, I reasoned it had to belong to Tony Grimes, and Will Grimes' house would be the next in line. Continuing another quarter mile, I came to a house I figured belonged to Will. It was one of the newer Mediterranean style homes.

I turned in, pulled up by the garage and stopped next to his white pickup. I glanced at Peggy Lou. She wiggled in her seat, eager to be released.

"Mommy needs to check something, honey," I said as I handed her another piece of apple. "I'll be right back."

I got out of the car and went over to the garage window, cupped my hands around my eyes and looked in. No yellow sports car.

He knew the area well and could have left the car in another location, maybe out in the orchard. I headed for the rear of the house to peek in windows to check for signs of life. I'd almost reached the back door when I saw something that brought me to a halt.

CHAPTER 34

Peeking out from under the back porch roof was a security camera, something I should have expected. Unless I wanted to do a lot of explaining to the local *gendarmes*, I figured I'd better forget about exploring inside Will Grimes' house. And I had to assume that Tony Grimes' home would be equipped in a similar manner. My snooping through the windows was squashed too. The blinds were all closed.

I returned to the Explorer and saw Peggy Lou squirming. I knew what that meant. As soon as I opened the car door, I heard, "Pee pee, Mommy."

"Hang on punkin'. Next stop, MacDonald's." I climbed in, pulled out onto the road and headed for Pelterville. It's a wonder I didn't get pulled over for speeding.

An hour later, after Peggy Lou had been pottied and fed, and had worked off some energy on MacDonald's playground equipment, we were almost to the turnoff to the Grimes Corporation headquarters. While watching her practice her climbing skill, I'd decided I would take a look around the Grimes' corporate grounds before visiting Vivian Rudd. With no obvious evidence that Will Grimes was hiding in his own house, it was the only logical place to look. Failing to locate him there, I'd need the family's cooperation to access his phone records, credit card charges, and bank statements.

I made the turn onto the long driveway leading to the office building, passed the branch that led to Vivian's house, and soon equipment buildings came into view. The parking spaces at the office were all empty, but in the distance, near the first row of walnut trees, a man in jeans and a green plaid shirt was closing the door on what looked like a tool shed. I pulled in, turned off the engine and watched as he placed a large metal box and a couple of shovels into the back of a white pickup, got in and guided it along the gravel lane that led past the office where I was parked. As he passed by, he waved and continued on down to the main road.

Quiet settled again. I sat and studied the buildings that undoubtedly held much of the equipment it took to manage the various crops the corporation grew and sent to market.

It seemed like a harebrained notion, but I supposed it was possible Will Grimes was holed-up in his own office. He could have returned after everyone had left the day before, perhaps thinking to destroy any evidence the investigators might have missed. But there was no sign of his car.

I looked around at Peggy Lou. It was her naptime and she was asleep. I got out and eased the door closed, then walked over to check the main door to the offices. As I expected, it was locked. Holly had been fired, Fillmore was in Arizona, and Will was…heaven knows where.

Walking to the east end of the building where the meeting had been held the previous day, I looked in the windows. I could see that someone, probably Tori, had removed the documents that had been on the table and repositioned the chairs. The hallway down the middle of the building was dark. I'd hoped the door to Will Grimes' office would be open and I'd see a light on. No such luck.

I went back to the SUV. Peggy Lou was still hugging her grubby toy kitten and peacefully napping, so I turned my attention to the equipment buildings located some fifty yards from where I stood. Though I doubted there was room for Grimes' car to be in any one of them, I decided to take a look anyway.

After a second glance at my daughter, I sprinted to the closest, a weather-worn barn. With a little effort on my part, the door creaked open. It was full of tractors and wagons that looked like they belonged in a museum. I pushed the door closed and went to the next structure, a steel building smaller than the barn. I pulled on the door handle and was surprised that it wasn't locked. Inside, I easily identified a repair shop with a work bench and a mechanic's tools laid out. A late-model tractor was parked in the middle.

The biggest of the buildings had the appearance of a more recent addition, a tan-colored warehouse with a matching enameled metal roof. It was locked. I hurried around to the window and had to stand on tip-toe to see the interior. One wall served to hold irrigation equipment, shelves with lengths of pipe and a row of bins I assumed contained parts for repairs. Along the back wall sat what looked like pumps, numerous rolls of black tubing and some cardboard boxes. A truck equipped with a tool box and pipe racks on either side was parked in the center.

I turned away and viewed a couple of open structures nearby, both empty, the equipment in use somewhere. I glanced in the direction of the Quonset hut hangars, the last possible location on the premises.

After another check on my daughter and seeing she continued to sleep, I pulled off the jacket I was wearing and hung it on the passenger side rearview mirror. Though the body holster and PPK were exposed, it felt better. The day was warming up.

The closest hangar held the wreckage of Tony Grimes' plane, but the other one, Fillmore's, would be empty since he was gone. I hurried over to it.

Anticipating that it would be locked like the other buildings, I didn't bother with the door. Instead, I focused on the window. The layer of dirt covering it was so thick I couldn't get a good view inside. I rubbed the glass with the heel of my hand, and was able to make out Will Grimes' yellow sports car. Bingo! It meant he *had* returned like I guessed, and was somewhere in the vicinity. I decided he had a screw loose if he thought he could hide the car there for very long. What was he thinking?

It was time to visit Vivian Rudd. Perhaps she would have some insight into her brother's state of mind. Or maybe she knew where he was all along. Was that why she was so anxious to talk to me? Had she gone home and found him there? If that were the case, why didn't she tell Claudine?

I put my jacket back on and got into the car, noticing the interior had warmed up too. I started the engine and rolled down the windows. The noise woke Peggy Lou. In the rearview mirror, I saw her straighten and drop her toy kitten. She struggled to catch it, and failed. "My kitty!" she bleated.

"I'll get it, sweetie," I said. Suppressing a little annoyance, I got out and walked around the car and opened the door. Wondering how long her attachment to the toy could go on, I retrieved it and handed it to her. Noticing her cheeks were flushed, guilt swept over me. Leaving a child sitting alone in a car is not a good idea. I pulled a bottle of water from the console and gave her a drink, then got back into the driver's seat. The temperature gauge on the dash read seventy-nine degrees. I tried to rationalize that I hadn't left her for more than a few minutes, but I couldn't make it stick. My adventure into being a working mother wasn't what I had imagined. I took a deep breath, decided to file those thoughts for a later time, and focus on questions I would ask Vivian Rudd.

CHAPTER 35

I pulled into the circular drive and parked next to the stone walk that led to the entrance of the handsome old house. It was a classic, two-story Craftsman home with square posts supporting each corner of the porch. Adding to its charm was the colorful rose garden that flanked the walkway. I got out of the SUV, stood for a moment and imagined the house dressed in the holiday decorations Torie had spoken of the day before.

"Mommy." Peggy Lou held out her arms to me. I opened the door, picked up the kitten again and helped her out. I grabbed her bag of toys and held her hand as we started up the half-dozen concrete steps that led to the front door. She pulled away and scampered up the steps like a monkey. I followed and pressed the doorbell. While we waited for someone to answer, I turned and gazed at the surrounding area. It was a pastoral scene, really, with the barns and sheds within view and the walnut orchard beyond.

Vivian Rudd soon responded, opening the door a crack. With recognition, she opened it wider. She was wearing blue denims and a man's shirt with the sleeves rolled up. Her eyelids were red, and she looked even more frail than the day before, cheeks sagging, her hair uncombed. She stared down at Peggy Lou as though I might have brought my dog along.

I said the obvious. "I have my daughter with me today."

She heaved a sigh. "Come in."

I took Peggy Lou's hand and stepped over the threshold into a foyer where a stairway to the right led to the upper floor.

"Claudine called me and said you were upset and wanted to speak to me."

"This way," Vivian said, leading us through a double-wide doorway. "We'll sit in the breakfast alcove. It'll be more comfortable than the parlor, and a more suitable place for a child."

As we followed her through the living room, I admired the features so typical of Craftsman homes: dark wood crown moldings, built-in cabinets, and pocket doors. The spacious living room was furnished with a sofa and chairs from the Arts and Crafts era, along with other pieces that likely had been in the family for generations. The stone fireplace was accented by a mantle made from a thick wooden plank.

I noticed family photos on the mantle and hesitated before moving on. One of them was of Vivian standing beside a small aircraft. She was very young, hair flowing over her shoulders and smiling at the camera as though proud of some accomplishment. Her pose reminded me of pictures I'd seen of Amelia Earhart. It triggered the memory of something Fillmore had said, causing bits and pieces of what I'd been hearing to come together into a conclusion I didn't like.

"Just through the dining room here," Vivian said.

Still a bit distracted by my own thoughts, I followed her and came into a country kitchen. In a windowed alcove on the left, three cushioned wicker chairs had been arranged on a flowered rug with a round table in the center. The table had been altered, the legs shortened, the level adjusted, making it lower than a standard table, but not as low as a coffee table. It was a cozy place to sit and have breakfast, or read, and be able to view the flower garden outside and the company buildings beyond.

Glancing around, I noticed two doors besides the one from the dining room. I assumed the one opposite the alcove was to the outside, and probably led to the garage I'd seen on that side of the house. The other, adjacent to the dining room door, I thought might be to a pantry or maybe a basement. Though the kitchen cabinets were a vintage design, stained dark, the appliances were modern. A butcher-block work table stood in the center of the room.

Vivian gestured to me to sit. "Would you prefer tea or coffee?"

"Coffee, please."

Peggy Lou climbed into one of the chairs, squirmed herself around and sat hugging her stuffed kitten. I sat in the next chair and placed my purse and the bag of toys on the floor next to my feet.

While the coffee perked, Vivian took a plate of cookies from one of the cabinets and brought it to the table. She took one of the cookies and leaned over to Peggy Lou. "What is your name?"

My daughter promptly held up three fingers and said, "Peggy Woo Wauker."

Vivian forced a smile. "That's a nice name." She handed her the cookie, set the plate down, then turned to me. "I imagine you brought something to amuse her while we talk."

I nodded and opened the toy bag. Peggy Lou scooted off the chair and looked inside. She took out a box of Crayons and a coloring book. With the book and colors in one hand and her kitten in the other, she plunked herself down on the rug, sat crossed-legged and opened the book.

Vivian returned to where the coffee pot sat on the counter, poured a cup and brought it to me. I took it, thanked her, took a sip and set it on the table. I had in mind getting right to the point. "I found your brother's car in the hangar over at the headquarters. He can't be thinking to keep it there very long. Fillmore will be returning tomorrow."

She sat in the wicker chair opposite me and folded her hands in her lap.

"Do you know where your brother is?"

She ignored me. "I think I should explain about Will, and what led to everything that has happened," she said. "I never thought it would turn out the way it did."

I took my mini-recorder out of my purse, placed it on the table, and pressed the button to start it. "I hope you don't mind me recording this, but I feel what you have to say is important."

She placed the tip of her finger on her lips and nodded.

I stated the date and place to have it on the tape in case it ended up in court.

"Has your brother been in touch with you since yesterday?"

She ignored me again.

"Will is sharp when it comes to business and marketing. He should be in control, not my nephew, and certainly not that woman Tony was going to marry. She's nothing but a gold-digger. She'd have sold out to those vultures at the Brookman Corporation. They'd have it all then. Everything would have been lost to the family."

She stared off into space and began lacing and unlacing her fingers the same way she had the day before.

"It wasn't fair. My father never treated Will like a son. Will had different talents. Father couldn't see that, and wouldn't listen to mother or me. It broke my mother's heart. I think it hastened her death. Just because he wasn't interested in guns and hunting and planes, it didn't mean he wasn't smart. My father invested his training in Tony, took him on business trips, introduced him to important people. Tony wasn't a fool. He lorded it over Will and played it for everything he could get. As my father aged, Tony was given more responsibility and control of the business. He was vested with even more power when the company incorporated. Father taught him everything about how to run an operation that size. That's why I had to do it."

I knew what she meant, but asked anyway. "Are you telling me you sabotaged your brother's plane?"

"It was the only way. Will just needed a chance to prove his ideas were right. Tony wouldn't listen to him, just like my father."

We sat quiet for a breath or two, her eyes gone liquid. "I'm a sick woman. I have pancreatic cancer. It doesn't matter what happens to me now."

I was formulating what I would say next when the back door jerked open with a gust of air. In stepped a hulk of a man in a sleeveless T-shirt, his arms covered with tattoos and his head shaved. For a split second, I didn't recognize him. But it was Buck Harper, all right, with a .38 special in his right hand.

With a sharp movement of her head, Vivian was suddenly indignant. She pushed out of her chair and swiveled in his direction, apparently not noticing the weapon. "What's the meaning of this? How dare you burst in here."

"Shut up," he bellowed, firing the revolver—pop! pop!

Vivian's hands flew to her chest. She collapsed in a heap between the chair and the table, blood trickling out from under her back onto the rug.

Adrenaline sent my pulse soaring.

He waved the gun at me. "Now you," he said. "Where's the money?"

"What money?"

"You know what money. The cash I stashed at Hester's. You two were tight. I saw it at the trial. You've moved it. Where is it?" He jabbed the gun in my direction, emphasizing his threat.

"I don't know what you're talking about." I kept my focus on him. I didn't dare move for fear he'd notice the bulge in my jacket and realize I was armed. "I never saw any money at Hester's. I was only in her house once."

"You're lying!" He stepped forward.

Peggy Lou, sitting on the rug, started whimpering. He looked at her as if it was the first he'd noticed a child in the room. With one long step, he grabbed her arm and jerked her to his side, then scooped her up, holding her with his left arm around her waist. I started to rise, my heart pounding in my chest.

"Stay!" he commanded, waving the gun at me.

"Mommy," she screamed, kicking and flailing her arms.

"Hold still, damn it," he said, looking down on her. Tightening his grip, he pointed the pistol at her head and looked at me. "Tell me where the money is, or she gets it."

"No! No! Mommy!" Peggy's desperate movements were making it hard to control her. It caused his grip to loosen. She slipped, still flailing, beating on his belly with her fists. He hitched her up for a better hold, but my daughter is a fighter. In the jostling, somehow, his gun hand came too close to her mouth. She bit into his skin. He let out a yowl, spewed curses and struggled to regain control.

In one swift motion, I reached inside my jacket, pulled out the PPK, released the safety, aimed at his head and fired. He pitched backward, his arms gone limp, and Peggy Lou crashed to the floor.

She shrieked, scrambled to her feet and into my arms, tears streaming down her cheeks. I laid my pistol on the table, leaned forward and folded my arms around her, both of us shaking and sobbing.

"What the hell's going on?" a male voice said. "That sounded like gun shots."

I was so startled I almost wet myself. Whirling around and groping for the pistol at the same time, I recognized Willard Grimes standing in the doorway to the basement.

EPILOGUE

It took several weeks for the aftermath to unfold. While the police dealt with the investigation, Buzz and I coped with how the experience affected Peggy Lou. Sleep was nearly impossible the first week. She'd wake screaming. Buzz or I had to sit and hold her until she could sleep again, sometimes for the remainder of the night.

In addition, she was terrified of any man who was not her father. We found a motherly child psychologist in Gateway, one who specialized in traumatized children. With weekly visits, her anxiety is beginning to resolve. In his career, Buzz had seen how children suffered after exposure to violence, so he took some time off to help us get through it.

In my case, the vision of Harper pointing his gun at her head filled my dreams. Sometimes I'd hear the final gunshot again and wake with a jerk. On the advice of the police psychologist, I've been receiving counseling too. When I asked Buzz if it was necessary, he said it couldn't do any harm, but then confessed he never agonized over pulling the trigger on someone like Harper.

I dreaded Madge's reaction when she heard about what happened. Though horrified, she didn't chide me for being involved in a risky business. The only thing she said was, "God forgive me, but I'm glad to hear that awful creature is dead. It's about time he stood before the Lord and accounted for his crimes." Madge had suffered at the hands of Buck Harper back when he broke into her house, whacked her on the head, and she ended up in the hospital thinking she was about to die.

After some thought, I decided to close the office. Until our daughter is acting like a normal kid again, my focus will be my family. With Buzz's assistance, we put the furnishings into storage, and I gave Bert a generous severance check. The owners of the building, local people, were very understanding and kind enough to release me from the rental agreement.

When it came to the police investigation, I had two things in my favor, the first being the tape recording of my conversation with Vivian. The tape continued running during the entire episode and gave them a pretty good picture of what happened. It turned out to be a bonus for them, answering the question of who had tampered with Tony Grimes' plane.

The other thing was that no one was particularly sorry about Buck Harper's demise. He'd been a thorn in law enforcement's side for years, starting when he was a teenager and he pistol-whipped a gas station attendant during a robbery. In the end, the District Attorney reviewed the case and deemed it justifiable homicide, which resulted in my PPK being returned to me.

I had several calls from reporters, Sheila Deiter being one of them. She wanted an exclusive interview. I turned her down. Irma called too. She thought she ought to come to the ranch to console me, considering my harrowing experience. What she really wanted was to hear all the juicy details. I managed to put her off.

A couple of weeks after the incident Claudine Morales phoned. Though stunned to learn of Vivian's confession on the recording, the death of their aunt served to deflate their acrimonious bubble. Grief stricken for the second time in a month, the family got together and talked sensibly for the first time in years. The result of the investigation into the corporate financial records showed no monies were actually missing. Will explained that the rancor between him and Tony had been caused by Tony's sinking enormous amounts of cash into the Arizona farms, in spite of his brother's protestations. That was the source of the argument the day of the crash.

The reason behind Will Grimes' vanishing act was that he'd figured out that Vivian was responsible for Tony's death. Since she knew about the structure and mechanics of an airplane due to her years of flying, he realized she had both the knowledge and opportunity to sabotage the control cables on Tony's plane. He knew about her cancer also, and was torn between his loyalty to her and his duty to report the crime. She'd been the person who'd always supported him, right or wrong, over the years. He was having a crisis of conscience and needed time to work it out.

Anything else? Oh yes, the money Harper was looking for. We concluded that he was the one who'd broken into Madge's garage, thinking I'd hid it there. The police scoured Hester's house for a third time, but nary a penny was found. My guess would be that one of his drug peddling buddies went looking for it while Harper was cooling his heels in prison.

It took me a little while to figure out how Harper tracked me to Vivian's house. Then it dawned on me that, like back in 1998, he'd planted a tracking device on my car, either that morning while it was parked at the office, or when I was busy with Peggy Lou at McDonald's. Buzz found it attached to the frame of my SUV.

He'd also stolen a Dodge van in Pelterville. After a call from Fillmore about a strange car the next day, the police found it parked over at the Corporation headquarters. During the follow-up, they learned he'd approached a guy in a parking lot at dawn, pushed the pistol in his face and told him he'd kill him if he didn't hand over the keys.

On a brighter note, a few days ago, Buzz came home with a surprise for us, a new puppy. The roly-poly bundle of fur delighted Peggy Lou from the first minute she saw him. Jeff wasn't as enthusiastic. He's been keeping his distance. But last night I noticed that the two of them had come to an agreement, each sleeping in his own corner of Peggy Lou's room. I think the pup has totally captured her affection. This morning I saw that the grubby stuffed kitten has been relegated to her toy box. I'll take it as a good sign.

As for myself, killing someone is not something I'd ever imagined doing, but it's part of me now, a detail of my life. Buzz understands, and so, in an odd sort of way, it's brought us closer.

ABOUT THIS AUTHOR

Gloria Getman, author of the *Deena Powers Mysteries*, spent 25 years as a registered nurse before following her bliss into writing fiction. She grew up in Southern California, graduated from California State University Bakersfield and lives in Exeter California, not far from Sequoia National Park. Her work has been featured in local publications as well as Yesterday's Magazette and Reminisce Extra. A few of her short stories can be found in the anthology, *Leaves from the Valley Oak*. She is a member of Tulare-Kings Writers, San Joaquin and Central Coast chapters of Sisters in Crime. Visit her at www.gloriagetman.blogspot.com

"These here two are gonna have a baby,"

Stephanie said, pointing to her and Skeeter. "And no grandchild of mine is gonna be born a bastard."

The skin on Lila's cheeks prickled with heat, and she wished with all her might she could just disappear. Skeeter started shouting. The rag over his mouth billowed and rough mumbles filled the room. The ropes binding him strained against his trouncing and his chair legs bounced a time or two.

"Is that true, Skeeter?" Kid asked angrily.

Skeeter started to mumble at the same time she jumped to his defense. Fighting the gag, as well as the thick rope wound around her, Lila tried to say none of it was Skeeter's doing, but between the rag and Skeeter's loud sounds, no one could understand her.

Kid held up one hand. "A simple yes or no is all I need."

"It's not his baby," Lila said against the cloth, shaking her head.

The older brother frowned, clearly not understanding what she'd said, and then glanced to Skeeter.

He mumbled beside her, long and loud the whole time gesturing with his head. Tails of the billowing white bow tied against his forehead fluttered and fell over his eyes. He flipped it aside, and Lila grimaced, afraid his wound would start bleeding again at his thrashing.

"Just nod your head," Kid said, staring at Skeeter. "Yes, she's going to have a baby? Or no, she's not?"

Simultaneously, she and Skeeter nodded their heads.

Praise for Lauri Robinson

... for BADLAND BRIDE, The Quinter Brides Book 2: "An amazingly well-woven story. ...a wonderful couple, but also a believable family. Skeeter is a charismatic, charming hero, and Lila is a great match for him. These characters are colorful, vibrant, and full of life. They surround you with their wit and realism.
~ *Author Mallary Mitchell*

...for SHOTGUN BRIDE, The Quinter Brides Book 1: "An uplifting novel, full of hope...I can't wait to read the sequels."
~ *Love Western Romances*

...for AN UNBELIEVABLE JOURNEY: "This story is captivating from start to finish."
~ *Robyn with Once Upon a Romance*

"I definitely recommend reading WIFE FOR BIG JOHN. I enjoyed it immensely and you will too!"
~*Laura of Two Lips Reviews, a Recommended Read*

...for MAIL ORDER HUSBAND: "I envision this book will be a keeper for many bookshelves; I highly recommend that you read it!"
~*Brenda Talley, The Romance Studio*